"I dare you to tell me what you're thinking right now," Megan said

Luke chuckled. "No problem. I was just thinking about what you'd look like when you came."

She gasped, which made him laugh. Heat shot through her.

He scooted closer to her, and once again they were touching from knee to hip. She swallowed. At least she didn't wonder where this was all headed. But despite the fact she'd come to his room, she wasn't about to tear off her clothes and shout, "Take me, big boy." Though the idea had appeal.

"Uh, your turn," she murmured, trying to get her brain cells to work. "Truth or dare?"

Luke rubbed her knee. "I *dare* you to tell me about your wickedest vacation fantasy."

"My what?"

"You know. We've all had them. Wild, crazy thoughts about what we'd do if there were no consequences. If all bets were off, and it was just about pure—" he leaned closer "—unadulterated—" his lips brushed her cheek as his warm breath slipped inside her without her permission "—sex."

Blaze™

To: My Favorite Reader
From: Jo Leigh
Subject: Men To Do!

Dear Reader,

We're back! Back with another Man To Do, and boy oh boy, is Luke Webster ever a hottie! He's pure sin and seduction, and what he does to Megan Hodges is definitely something to write home about.

I loved writing this book.... Luke has so many of the qualities I love in a man. As for Megan? She's like me in so many ways...full of contradictions. She's strong at work, but on unsteady ground when it comes to love. She's a great friend, a smart cookie, a real go-getter, and yet she's not at all sure that she's worthy of the love Luke has to offer. I hope you identify with her, too.

As for me, I'm enjoying my own romance, which has made writing this Blaze novel a real, um, experience. All that research, you know. <wink>

Have fun, and don't forget to come play at www.mentodo.com.

Best,

Jo Leigh

Books by Jo Leigh

HARLEQUIN BLAZE

2—GOING FOR IT
23—SCENT OF A WOMAN
34—SENSUAL SECRETS
72—A DASH OF TEMPTATION*

*Men To Do

TRUTH OR DARE

Jo Leigh

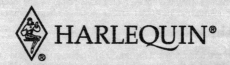

HARLEQUIN®

TORONTO • NEW YORK • LONDON
AMSTERDAM • PARIS • SYDNEY • HAMBURG
STOCKHOLM • ATHENS • TOKYO • MILAN • MADRID
PRAGUE • WARSAW • BUDAPEST • AUCKLAND

To LWW
for the inspiration and the love

ISBN 0-373-79092-9

TRUTH OR DARE

Copyright © 2003 by Jolie Kramer.

This edition published by arrangement with Harlequin Books S.A.

® and TM are trademarks of the publisher. Trademarks indicated with
® are registered in the United States Patent and Trademark Office, the
Canadian Trade Marks Office and in other countries.

Visit us at www.eHarlequin.com

Printed in U.S.A.

1

THE MODEL—Megan Hodges thought her name was Trisha—peeled off her shirt to reveal two large, gravity-defying, naked breasts perched on a body so slim one could play her ribs like a xylophone. She then picked up a pale blue, cashmere sweater, and slipped that on instead. The whole operation lasted about a minute, and would have been wholly unremarkable except for the fact that Trisha was smack-dab in the middle of thirty-seven strangers—men, women and a few who defied classification. No one gave the breasts a second glance.

While millions of pubescent males would have spiked granny's prune juice to get a load of those bare boobs, to Megan and her compatriots they were incidental. As interesting as the apples on the craft service table. Not worth mentioning unless they were actually in the shot. Even then, they weren't looked at as *breasts*. Nothing sexy or sensual or fun. They were as glamorous as teeth.

Such was the fashion business, and even Megan, who'd only been working for the House of Giselle for six months, was jaded to the point of boredom when it came to body parts. Other people's body parts, that is. Her body parts were an entirely different issue.

Megan had been in love with fashion forever. She'd drawn clothes from the moment she could hold a crayon. She'd read everything ever written about Coco Chanel, studied *Vogue* as if it were the Bible, dreamed glorious dreams of being the next Vera Wang, Versace or even Stella McCartney. Fashion design was her all, her reason, her passion.

The only drawback was that in order to pursue her dream of becoming a world famous designer, she had to actually work in the fashion industry.

And the fashion industry, Megan had realized as far back as freshman year at New York University, was about facades. That might have sounded obvious, but Megan had never viewed fashion that way. To her, clothing was an expression of self, a way of showing on the outside the truth of what was inside. Only, as far as she could tell, no one in the fashion industry had anything interesting on the inside, so there went her theory.

Okay, so maybe that wasn't fair. She had met a few people who actually bothered to scratch the surface, but they were young, like her. She had no doubt that by the time their various apprenticeships were over, they'd be as cynical and shallow as the designers they emulated. It would happen to her, too. Eventually.

Who was she kidding? There was no eventually. It was her second year as a design assistant, first year working for Damian Croft, the force behind Giselle, and she'd already succumbed to the awful, horrible, disgusting habit of dismissing the poorly dressed without so much as a how-do-you-do. Not all the time. But more often than she should.

She should know better, which was the understatement of the year. But she'd been seduced by the dark side. The photographers who bitched if the models had an ounce of flesh on their emaciated bodies. The designers who wanted hangers, not humans, to wear their creations. The models themselves who lived and died by the calorie. All of whom ignored her with an indifference perfected to an art form.

Megan leaned back on her director's chair and stretched her neck for a few moments while she waited for Damian to check the lighting. Her gaze fell to her pad where she'd been sketching a winter coat. She was supposed to be sketching random ideas flung out like chum on the water, that she would catch and make real via the magic of her charcoals. Only Damian hadn't had an idea all day, and she was bored beyond endurance.

The thought of walking out the door and never looking back caught her fancy, but only for a moment. Never one to be deterred by anything so mundane as reality, Megan was on a mission. She was going to change things. Not just with her designs but with her attitude.

Damian threw something small and hard, probably his lens, across the set and stormed off, probably to his trailer to do a few lines of coke. Which meant she wasn't going to be busy for at least another hour. Plenty of time to pull her laptop out of her backpack and check her e-mail. The girls at Eve's Apple, her online reading group, had been discussing *Sex and the City,* and while Megan wanted to be like Samantha, she was disarmingly like Charlotte. Actually,

Charlotte was braver. More confident. Prettier by a mile.

Which didn't mean Megan hated everything about herself. She had great hair. Everyone said so, and even if they hadn't she would still have loved her hair. It was long, down past her shoulders, and brown, but with so much red it glistened. It was thick, too, and straight, but she could make it behave with her round brushes and hair dryer. One perk to working this job was that she had access to hair and makeup experts, and if they were sufficiently bored, they would give her hints and tips.

For the most part, she was satisfied with her body. She wasn't too skinny or too fat, she had pretty nice B-cups that didn't sag, and her ass wasn't grotesquely huge or anything. No, she'd have been really content with her looks if it wasn't for the leg.

The leg. The damn leg. The brace that looked like something from a medical horror movie. The atrophy which had made that leg so much thinner than the other, despite the exercises she did on a daily basis, which, by the way, hurt like a mother. The leg that made her limp, that forced her to wear long skirts and baggy slacks. The leg that made her different. Flawed. Other.

On good days, it didn't bother her at all. On bad days, it made her want to scream. The thing was, despite all the evidence of her own life, and everyone else's that she knew of personally, Megan still believed in the philosophy of fairness: If you work hard, you'll be rewarded. If you're nice, nice things will happen to you.

Only, the people she knew who truly were successful in this business weren't nice, didn't do nice things and they were rewarded up the ying-yang. And she knew way too many women who worked their tails off and still got a quarter of what they were worth.

As far as the leg and fairness went… Hell, there was no fairness at all.

She settled her laptop on her lap and turned it on, the familiar baritone voice announcing that she had mail. She deleted a ton of spam, then opened up the good stuff. As she read the letters from this group of bright women from all over the country, she relaxed more and more, until finally she felt comfortable in her chair, in the room. But one e-mail held her interest in a way none of the others had.

Denise, who had belonged to Eve's Apple longer than anyone except for Samantha, Erin and Tess, had written about a little experiment that the founding members had instituted. A little gem called Men To Do. Actually, the official title was Men to Do Before You Say I Do, but MTD was easier to type.

It was very simple, and quite clever. You find a guy you wouldn't marry, wouldn't even want to take home to mom and dad; the kind of guy you dream about when the night is too long and the bed too big. The kind of guy who was just scary enough, or just weird enough, or too good-looking to have any kind of manageable ego: movie stars, biker dudes, playboys, boy toys.

Once you've found your MTD, you do him. And do him. Shamelessly. Greedily. Joyfully. When you're through, you say buh-bye, and that's that. You're ready to get serious. Get real. Get hitched. Or not. But you'll always have that memory of the time you were in control, you were in the captain's seat, you were…like Samantha on *Sex and the City.*

Megan sent her own e-mail to the group, just a short note to say she'd write later, after she'd given this thing some thought. Then she closed her laptop and grabbed her thermos instead. After pouring herself a still steaming cup of chai, she leaned back for some major thinking.

This idea intrigued her greatly. It also scared her spitless. The concept was faboo…find Brad Pitt-George Clooney-Ben Affleck and wear him out in the bedroom Olympics, then move on. Only, one would have to get Brad Pitt-George Clooney-Ben Affleck to agree to the program. Yeah. Uh-huh. Like that was going to happen to her.

On the other hand, maybe her MTD wouldn't have to be of the movie-star-looks persuasion. Maybe her guy could be someone in the scary category. A Hell's Angel. A race car driver. A boxer.

She sipped her tea, letting the sweet brew warm her insides. It's not as if she hadn't ever dated before. She had. Plenty of times. Despite her gimpitude, she wasn't a total pariah. Of course, she hadn't had much luck with any true hotties, but she'd met some nice guys.

However, nice guys were not Men To Do.

And the leg would surely stop any bona fide babe in his tracks.

What to do… What to do???

"ARE YOU HIGH?"

Megan didn't dignify the question with an answer.

In any event, June didn't give her an opening for a response.

"First of all, you don't ski, so when people ask you how you broke your leg, what are you going to say? Second, if you do end up meeting your man to whatever, it won't be any good because you'll be lying to the guy from the start."

"May I speak now?"

June scowled, then took a big bite out of her onion bagel. Friends since art school, June had been the yin to Megan's yang for five years. Megan had moved into June's building seven months ago when the apartment on the fifth floor had opened up. It was small, even by New York standards, but it was cheap, at least for New York. Eight hundred a month, including utilities. Cable was an extra fifty, the phone averaged fifty and groceries were another two hundred. Not bad on her illustrator's salary.

While not much was left over, Megan and June had become connoisseurs of thrift stores, flea markets and estate sales. Most weekends, they'd be out scavenging for anything interesting, not just for fun, but as a major source of income.

June had discovered eBay, and she did a nice business reselling other people's junk. Of course they didn't have room in either of their apartments to store the trinkets and treasures, but June had circumvented that little obstacle by using the basement at her Uncle Sid's appliance store. Uncle Sid had stopped selling appliances four years ago, but he still fixed them. These weren't your Kenmore refrigerators or Whirlpool washers. Sid was the master of the discontinued model, the off-brand, the dinosaurs that had no business being fixed at all.

Sid loved what he did, and due to some wise investments when the store actually did sell new units, he could spend his days, his weeks, finding replacement parts and matching paint chips. Since not that many people in New York had antique stoves, the basement of his building had enough empty space for June to store her booty.

She had a knack, undoubtedly inherited from Sid himself, of finding old things and giving them new life. Lamps that needed a new plug, purses with a few missing beads, clothes that needed a nip or tuck to turn from merely old to vintage. Megan did most of the sewing, of course, and June took care of the rest. The cream of the crop always ended up in one of their apartments, which meant the decor was ever-changing and, to put it mildly, eclectic. Case in point was the chair June occupied. Not a bad reproduction of a Shaker chair, currently painted a rich, dark purple. Which wasn't as bad as it seemed, given that Megan's living room had a great many purple accessories, from a macaroni shell lampshade to several hand sewn pillows. Purple was Megan's signature color.

''I still think it's a bonehead idea,'' June said.

''We're talking about six days. That's all. Not the rest of my life. Six days where I can be just like everyone else. Can't you see that?''

''You're not like everyone else. Why would you want to be? Most people are jerks.''

Megan looked down at her leg, the ugly brace like something Torquemada might have cooked up on a dull afternoon. "I figured you'd understand," she said. "It's unrelenting, you know. Every day, every step. It matters, and I hate it, and I want a damn break. I don't care if I meet a man to whatever or not. I want..."

June got up from the couch and walked over to the overstuffed chair where Megan sat, holding a pillow to her tummy. Not purple though. Candy apple red. "Hey. I'm sorry. I don't mean to sound like the bitch who ate Queens, but damn, girl, this smells dangerous to me. I'm not talking about meeting an ax-murderer or anything. I'm talking about walking in shoes that don't belong to you."

Megan looked up. June had her wild copper hair pulled back into a mess of a ponytail. Her odd assortment of necklaces glittered with the light from the halogen lamp. Megan saw the concern on her face, the worry in her pale green eyes. "I need to do this," she said. "Just to see."

"See what?"

Megan shook her head. "I don't know. I can't explain it. To see what it's like."

"Megan, honey, that's just it. What if it's wonderful?"

"Please don't ruin this for me. Please?"

June frowned. "Okay. Jeez. So Darlene said she'd do the cast, right?"

Megan grinned. "Yep. It's synthetic, so I can get it wet. It's lighter, too."

"What's the cast going to do to your leg?"

"Nothing. It'll be like wearing the brace, only all the time. I'll be fine."

"Have you ever been to a ski lodge?"

Megan shook her head.

"I hope you know what you're doing."

"I've got a month to think about it. Although I can't imagine changing my mind."

"Ha! As if you've ever changed your mind."

"I'm tenacious," Megan said.

"Stubborn."

"Committed."

"Pigheaded."

"Yeah, well, I love you, too."

"Shit." June went to the front door. "I'm making mac and cheese. Want some?"

"You betcha."

"Fake casts. Men to do." June mumbled as she headed out. "And people say I'm nuts."

LUKE WEBSTER stepped out onto Pearl, joining the stream of brokers and traders leaving the Wall Street offices for the night. He'd had a tough day with the news about Genco's Chapter 11, but he'd covered his assets and made some of his clients a nice piece of change. Still, he was bushed.

One more week, and then he could get the hell out of Dodge. He needed a break. To get out in the cold air and the soft packed snow and burn off some energy. He had the new Atomic skis to break in, and he intended to give them a real workout.

The weather reports in Mountain Creek all looked good. He'd booked the suite at the resort for six days, five nights. Five nights with, if all went well, five different women. Each one a beautiful bundle of hot, wet surprises. God, he loved the winter.

He made his way to the curb and held out his arm

for a cab. It took almost fifteen minutes to snare one, which was typical of a Wednesday night. If it rained, the wait would have been more like thirty, but the sky was clear, the stars were bright, and he had a cold beer waiting for him at the apartment.

The cabby was blessedly content to keep quiet and listen to the Rasta station on his front seat boom box as he maneuvered through rush hour traffic. Luke laid his head back on the vinyl seat and closed his eyes, visualizing his first grand slalom run. He'd just bought some of the sweetest-turning slalom skis he'd ever seen. They'd cost a fortune, but they were worth it.

A horn, loud enough to wake the dead, shook him from his reverie, and he sat up. Shit, he was still twenty blocks from home, and 74th was a parking lot. He got out his wallet, paid the man, then climbed out of the cab. He'd hoof it, maybe stop at the gym on the way. He'd worked out this morning, but a few laps around the track wouldn't hurt.

Besides, there was a new aerobics instructor he hadn't met yet. Tall, tight and tan, she would look damn good with those legs wrapped around his waist. His pace quickened as he focused on getting to the gym. The crowd on the street became a welcome challenge as he ducked and dodged, feinted and pushed. He made it in seven minutes.

2

THE LODGE was as beautiful as a postcard. The three-story A-frame was decorated in rustic charm, although Megan wasn't sure there was ever a real reason to have antlers as an ornament, even if they were acting as chandeliers. The centerpiece of the great room was the stone fireplace, big enough to roast an elk, if one were inclined. Mostly, it just crackled with a jolly fire, warming the snow bunnies and a quite generous selection of hunky snow babes, all within yodeling distance of Megan's wing chair.

Her leg, casted with dexterity and verve by Megan's neighbor, looked good on the overstuffed ottoman. No one without an X-ray machine would be able to detect that while her leg was mangled, it wasn't broken. She'd already gotten several sympathetic comments from the wait staff as they brought her cocoa, mulled cider and a Bailey's and coffee, respectively.

It was crowded where she sat, adjacent to the bar, across from the large dining room, kitty-corner to the registration desk. Her view was only impeded by the fireplace, but since the après-ski crowd seemed eager to circulate, that wasn't a problem.

She'd gotten more attention about her sketch pad than her cast, which surprised her. Everyone who stopped seemed surprised that she could draw, that her figures were recognizable, that she was, as one perky blonde in a sweater several sizes too small had put it, "totally awesome."

Megan had grown accustomed to the supreme indifference of the fashion crowd, who expected "totally awesome" work as the given. Before, during and shortly after art school, she'd taken her sketch pad everywhere, and had inspired many a fascinating conversation from impromptu models or passersby. Of course, she'd also inspired a startling number of rude comments, indecent proposals and three actual flashers. Her favorite had been the one at Rockefeller Center. He'd gone the raincoat route...so unimaginative. He'd bared himself to her, wagging his hips as he leered, and she had simply looked up, shook her head and said, "Hmm, that looks like a penis, only smaller." The flasher had retreated with his tail, as it were, between his legs. The elderly couple on the bench next to hers had applauded. It was all in the timing, and traditionally, Megan thought of the bon mot two hours after the perfect opportunity presented itself.

She sipped her drink, adjusted her leg using both hands, unaccustomed to the weight of the cast, then took another gander at the crowd.

She'd done well with her wardrobe selection, she felt. A burgundy sweater that hugged her B-cups but didn't strain, jeans with one leg cut off just above the cast, moccasins over warm, wooly socks, and a nice roomy leather tote, courtesy of a photo shoot three months ago and a generous wardrobe mistress.

She'd taken care with her hair and makeup, which

is something she didn't normally do. When everyone stared at her legs, why bother? But her overall plan had merit, she'd seen that during the past few hours. She was one of the crowd, she blended, and the only sympathy she got had a certain camaraderie that warmed her more than the fire.

Even if she didn't get her Man To Do, she would know it wasn't because she was a gimp. Which was actually a bit scary, as it would mean she wasn't attractive even without the brace. But she wouldn't think about that. Not on her first night. Not when she was just beginning to feel the Bailey's and there were so many pretty, pretty boys all around. God, perfect asses lovingly cradled in spandex…proof positive there was a benevolent higher power.

One ass in particular caught her attention. It rode high on long, muscular—but not bulging—legs, topped with slender hips and a package, if one could believe the silhouette, of heroic proportions. Her gaze moved up, lingering on the vee of a broad chest, covered in a sweater that Megan would bet was made of excellent cashmere. His jaw made her pause, as it was squared and masculine, perfectly symmetrical, as were his lips. Even his nose, slightly crooked, slightly larger than she'd have guessed, was perfect. If his eyes were as beautiful…

They were. Dark, heavily lashed, they intrigued even from a distance. One hand cleared her old sketch and bared a new page while the other gripped her charcoal and while she stared, not even glancing down at her fingers, she drew, wanting to catch the shadow above his upper lip, the strong cheekbones, but mostly the humor in his eyes.

His laughter distracted her for a moment, such a deep, rich sound that she had to smile, but then her fingers started moving again, and she had him in her mind's eye. Her gaze shifted to the page, filling in lines and shadows, creating flow and form from contrast.

This was her space, private, intimate in a crowd, magical as the image sharpened, became lifelike, animated. She'd love to draw forever, never be without paper and pencil, always looking for an intriguing line or a bold challenge.

She caught the curve of his jaw, the shell of his ear, and the music from behind the bar dimmed and was replaced by a private melody that she hummed quietly.

The man, the babe, she'd found so attractive became more than what he was. Pure in a way that only art can conjure. Lines, circles, shadow, light. Joy somewhere deep in her soul, where she wasn't clumsy or different. Megan was hardly there in the lodge. She'd been transported by beauty. Set up on wings.

"I'm flattered."

The masculine voice cut her flight and she landed back in her chair with a start. Swiveling her head around to her right, heat crawled up her neck as she saw the man, the babe, staring over her shoulder.

"You're very talented," he said.

Her cheeks heated further with the compliment, and she fought the foolish urge to hide her drawing with her arm. She hadn't done anything wrong. He didn't seem upset. Yet, she felt exposed, as if he'd caught her with her pants down.

"I'm Luke," he said, walking around her wing chair until he stood slightly to the right of the otto-man. "Luke Webster."

Despite the dryness of her mouth, she managed, "Megan Hodges."

"What happened?" he asked, nodding to her leg.

"Skiing accident."

"Damn, that's a shame. I hope it isn't too bad."

"I'll recover," she said, wincing a bit at the lie. "Thank you."

He looked around for a moment, then back at her. "No free chairs. Mind if I share?" He indicated the ottoman with a glance.

"No. Of course not." She lifted her cast, shifting it to the side to give him room. The adjustment gave her a moment to compose herself, even though a moment wasn't nearly enough.

Up close he was more gorgeous than she had imagined, and she had a damn good imagination. His eyes were deep blue, ocean-blue, interested, quick. The square jaw that had first caught her eye lost its harshness with the quirk of his slight smile. She'd gotten his body right, though. Tall, well over six feet, broad of shoulder, slim of hips, he was an athlete—toned, taut, vibrating with health. He reminded her of the models she saw so often, yet he seemed more than pretty. There was intelligence in his gaze, curiosity, too.

"You're an artist," he said, as he sidled right up to her leg. "Professional or is it a hobby?"

She wasn't ready for this. It was too soon, and he was too gorgeous, and oh, God, he couldn't possibly be her Man To Do, could he? Him? With his sable lashes and wavy brown hair? There were so many beautiful women in the lounge, he could have his pick. Even as he waited for her response she could see a redhead wearing skintight overalls giving him the once-over, and next to her, a brunette who looked like a strong breeze would topple her forward eyed him with barely concealed interest.

"Professional," she said, finally, turning her attention back to Luke. "I work for a fashion designer in the city."

His brow arched with interest. "No kidding. I don't know many people in that industry. Must be interesting."

"I like it, although it's not nearly as glamorous as one would hope."

"In my experience, glamour is overrated. I'd rather get real satisfaction from my work than have the trappings."

"What do you do?"

"Stockbroker," he said.

"And do you get the satisfaction you desire?"

"Sometimes. With the market so volatile these days, it keeps me on my toes."

"I'll bet."

He smiled, creating a flurry of butterfly action in her tummy. "Don't worry. I make it a point to avoid all conversations about my work with those on the outside. I get tired of watching people's eyes glaze over."

What she wanted to tell him was that he could read the phone book to her, and she wouldn't be bored. Instead, in her best, most casual, voice, she said, "I admit I don't know much about the stock market, but

I don't find it dull. I would imagine it takes someone quite clever to succeed.''

"Thank you. I think I will change the subject, so you won't have to adjust your view.''

She smiled, practiced her coy look-away. "Okay, then what do you talk about, when you don't talk about work?''

"Sports, mostly. Participating, not watching.''

Megan's heart sunk. Great. A jock. Of course, she had no business expecting anything else. People didn't come to the lodge to read. She hadn't realized until just this second that while she'd wanted her Man to Do to be jocklike, she hadn't really wanted him to be a jock. Another example of her impeccable perception and exquisite planning. "Sports? As in different ones?''

He nodded. "A few.''

"For instance?''

"Skiing, of course. Snowboarding. In the summer I like to sail and do some diving. What about you?''

"Well, I haven't done a lot of sailing or diving, although it sounds wonderful. And I don't know one end of a snowboard from the other. So, I guess that leaves skiing.''

"Skiing is enough. Unless you're out of commission.''

"Yeah," she said, trying to sound chagrined. "Just my luck.''

"How long are you here for?''

"Six days, five nights.''

"I suppose you can't get your money back?''

"Nope.''

"So what are you going to do for the rest of your stay?"

"Well, everyone here can't ski all the time."

He laughed, but she didn't care because his hand was on her leg. Well, not exactly on her leg, but on her cast, which was on her leg, and even though she couldn't feel it, she could imagine what he felt like. Warm. Strong. Big hands. Whoa, yeah.

"Megan?"

Her gaze snapped back to him and she felt a blush start at her chest and move up. "Sorry. Distracted momentarily."

"Did I hurt you?" he said, removing his hand, causing her great disappointment.

"No, not at all. But it still feels funny, you know? A little itchy. Warm."

"Been there. It sucks." He looked around the room, and Megan's disappointment swelled. He was done with her. Of course. On to bigger and brighter things. Ski babes. Model types. Ambulatory women.

Luke finished his sweep of the room and he once again looked at her. "You have dinner yet?"

She blinked as she shifted gears. "No."

"Want to?"

"Uh, sure."

"Great. Tell you what. You wait here while I get a table. I'll come back for you, okay?"

"Uh, sure."

He stood, gave her a crooked half grin, then headed left. That meant he was going to the steak house. Not the café. Cool.

She took a deep calming breath, then panicked. She only had a few minutes here to get her act together. Hell, that could take years. But she'd have to make do with putting her charcoal away, folding up her drawing pad, running a hand through her hair, freshening up her lipstick and checking to make sure she had no black gunk in the corners of her eyes. Once her makeup bag was back in her purse, she started to get up, but realized quickly that she had to think this maneuver through.

First, the leg in the cast had to come down from the ottoman. God, it weighed a ton. Worth it, though. It looked absolutely genuine. And it had worked. She couldn't wait to call June and tell her. June, who'd doubted her plan, who'd cast aspersions on her intelligence. Who'd predicted nothing but failure and heartache. Ha! First night here, and she'd scored! Okay, well, not scored in the biblical sense, but damn. Luke was quite possibly the best-looking man in the lodge, and he'd chosen her for a dinner companion.

It *was* the leg. She'd known it all along. The leg and the brace just plain scared the bejesus out of guys, that's all.

Not that that was the best news, come to think of it. The cast was only hers on loan. Once home, she'd have to go back to being a gimp. And that meant being alone.

However, in true Scarlett O'Hara fashion, she wasn't going to think about that tonight. She had dinner plans.

She reached for her crutches, putting all thoughts of the real world away for the duration.

LUKE HAD GIVEN the maître d' a twenty for a decent table, one that would be easy for Megan.

She was interesting. Not his typical ski companion. Aside from the broken leg. He probably wouldn't have even noticed her if it hadn't been for the drawing.

She was incredibly talented, even he could see that. She'd caught him on that pad of hers, in a way that took him aback. More than even a photograph, she'd captured his… She'd captured something. Now that he thought about it, he wasn't at all sure what. A feeling? An attitude? He couldn't say, except that it was true, and it wasn't something most people saw.

But he wasn't having dinner with her because she could draw. He liked her smile. Her laugh. In fact, he had the feeling the rest of the night was going to be great. A hell of a start to his week of wine, women and skiing.

He rounded the corner, and there she was, standing next to the big old wing chair. Leaning on her crutches. Poor kid. Bad luck. But she didn't seem too devastated by the turn of events. Good for her.

"I was going to help you," he said.

"No need. At least, not at the moment. How did it go at the restaurant?"

"Our table awaits."

"Excellent."

He stood at her side. If she hadn't had crutches, he would have taken her hand. But he had to settle for resting his palm on the small of her back as they headed for the restaurant.

He wished she wasn't wearing a sweater. That was the problem with winter. Too many damn clothes.

"Is this your first time here?" she asked, glancing at him.

"Nope. It's the closest decent skiing to Manhattan, so I'm up here a couple of times a season."

"I noticed that earlier. How most of the people here are New Yorkers."

"The resort makes it pretty attractive to come here. Discounts on lifts and rooms, that kind of thing. You'll have to come back when you can really enjoy it."

"I'm having a pretty good time now."

"That's all that matters."

"I like to think so."

He smiled as they got to the steak house entrance. The maître d' led them to the table, then handed them the menus as he helped Megan with her crutches. By the time she was settled, water had been poured, and the waiter stood by.

"Do you want some wine?"

She nodded. "Sure."

"A Merlot okay?"

"Great."

Luke nodded at the waiter.

"It won't be a moment, sir."

Luke turned his attention to Megan. "You comfy?"

She nodded. "Comfy and hungry."

He handed her a menu. "Me, too," he said, although he didn't even glance down. He was far more interested in the woman across from him than the entrées.

If he had to guess, he'd say she was in her mid-twenties, which was young, but not ridiculously so.

He liked her hair, a lot. It wasn't all fancy or anything, just shiny and dark with red highlights and he'd bet it was soft as new-fallen snow. She tucked it behind her ears, but left a few tendrils loose to soften her cheeks. Her eyes were big, brown and sexy. They crinkled up when she smiled, and he liked that. He liked her smile, too. Nice teeth. Good bones. Healthy. He'd wager she was a damn good skier when she wasn't banged up.

"I can't decide," she said.

"What?"

"I'm thinking the filet looks good. But the wasabi salmon sounds really interesting."

"I'll get the filet, you get the fish and we'll share. But I'm having the chocolate cake for dessert, and if you want some, you'll have to order it because I don't share chocolate cake."

She gave him an odd little grin. "Fair enough."

"What's wrong?"

"Nothing."

"Come on. What's that look?"

"You surprise me, that's all."

"How?"

"I'm not sure I can spell it out. You're a stockbroker. A jock. A yuppie from Manhattan."

"Yuppie? I didn't think there were yuppies anymore. But I digress."

Her grin broadened. "See you did it again."

"What?"

"Surprised me."

"In a good way, I hope."

"Oh, yeah."

"Then I'm down with it." He put his menu aside

and stretched his legs out under the table. He was comfortable, relaxed. Like he was with a friend.

"So, tell me," she said.

"Tell you what?"

"Everything. Childhood, college, life in Manhattan. You know. The works."

"Jeez, I don't know. That could take some time."

"I'm a captive audience. I can't escape very easily, even if I wanted to."

"Hmm." He waggled his brows suggestively. "That does give one pause."

She blushed. Her cheeks got pink and she glanced everywhere but at him.

"You're something of a surprise yourself. I mean, a fashion illustrator from Manhattan, blushing like a schoolgirl. Go figure."

"I haven't been in the big bad city long enough to have lost my little town ways."

"What little town would that be?"

"Chicago."

He laughed. "Megan, my girl, I think I was very wise to investigate the woman with the charcoal."

"I hope so."

She stopped talking as the waiter came by with the wine. They went through the opening ceremonies with no disappointments. Once they were alone again, he sipped some Merlot and thought about where to begin. "I grew up in Los Angeles," he said. "My father had a hardware store on Sepulveda Boulevard. We lived upstairs from the store."

"Brothers? Sisters?"

"I have two younger brothers, Jack and Michael.

Jack's in college back in L.A. and Michael's a plumber.''

"How did you end up in New York?"

"College. I went to Rutgers."

"That's in New Jersey, right?"

He nodded. "Damn good school."

"So I've heard."

"What about you?"

"Art school. In New York."

"You were probably the valedictorian of your class, am I right? Definitely the best artist."

"Ah, you ᴉᴇ sweet, but no, far from it. But I did love it there. I was lucky to get in."

"Were you on the scholarship train?"

She nodded.

"Me, too."

"I loved being in college. It was everything I'd imagined. Scary, but good scary."

"I could have done without finals just fine," he said. "But yeah, it was good."

"So, you live in the city now, and work on Wall Street?"

"Talk about scary."

"I can only imagine. That huge room, all that yelling and tension."

"No, I was talking about the subways."

She laughed, and he liked the sound of it. Liked what happened to her eyes.

"I'm one of those nuts who likes the subway," she said. "There's no place on earth better to watch people."

"Ah, you've seen one guy peeing in a trash can, you've seen 'em all."

"Okay, I grant you, there are some unpleasant things down there, but it's more interesting than that. I mean, I've seen every kind of person. Young, old, rich, poor. I've seen fantastic faces."

"You see a different subway. I think I'd like to see it from your perspective."

"Try bringing a drawing pad some time."

"I don't think so. I can't even do stick figures well. It's embarrassing."

"You probably haven't ever been taught, that's all."

"Naw, I suck. Trust me."

"I'm lousy at stocks and bonds, so we're even."

"I bet you're a demon on skis."

"Demon? I don't think so."

He narrowed his eyes knowingly. "I have a sixth sense about these things. I can tell when someone is courageous."

"Like those guys who jump out of helicopters and outrun avalanches?"

"I said courageous, not insane."

"Okay, then."

He leaned forward planting his elbows on the table. "Don't get me wrong. I don't have a death wish. But while I'm alive, I have no intention of sitting back and watching it from the sidelines. I can't imagine a worse fate."

Her heart bumped in her chest. She wondered what he'd say if he knew what was underneath her cast. "Some people have to watch. They can't do."

"There's always something you can do. Some way to step outside the safety zone. Most people are so afraid, they live little, tiny lives. They let television live for them.''

She needed to get off this topic before she burst out crying. ''You mean you don't watch *Days of Our Lives?* What kind of rinky-dink college did you go to?''

He sat back, in his chair, prepared to lie through his teeth, then decided, what the hell. ''Okay. So I watched a few soap operas in the common room. So shoot me.''

''I'll let it go this time.''

''It wasn't *Days of Our Lives,* by the way.'' He looked at the table next to theirs, then lowered his voice. ''*General Hospital.*''

Her grin faded. ''You didn't.''

''I did. But in my defense, it wasn't up to me. There was a general vote.''

''Hmm. I guess it's all right then.''

''Tell me the truth, Megan, do you still…?''

''Nope. Not once since I graduated. Odd, how that's become such a ritual though, huh? Watching soaps?''

''I think it's because students need to find someone who's life is in worse shape than their own.''

''True,'' she said.

The food came, and the conversation slowed, but only until the portions were meted out, and the initial tasting ended.

''Good plan,'' she said, stabbing another piece of steak. ''I like.''

''You do, huh?''

She nodded. ''That's one thing I didn't get caught

up in at college. The vegetarian thing. Although I probably should have. It does seem healthier.''

''Oh, don't even get me started. I'm a carnivore. I make no apologies.''

''Cool.'' She grinned again, and ate some more of her dinner. It was a refreshing change to see a woman chow down on her potato and even the bread on the table. Most women he dined with had lettuce with no dressing. It was depressing. Megan, however, had the kind of appetite that gave him hope. Lettuce eaters, although usually beautiful, if not too thin, tended to be timid in the bedroom, too. Too aware of their own bodies to really let go. He didn't think Megan would have that problem.

The idea of finding out took root. Not that he hadn't thought of it before, but that was just in passing. Sort of like scratching an itch. Now, he realized, he needed to focus. To plan. To conquer. ''It's your turn,'' he said.

''My turn to what?''

''Tell me your life story.''

''Wait a minute. You're not finished. I know you ski. And probably a number of other daredevilish things. And I know you trade. But that's just the top layer.''

He gave her a worried look. ''What do you mean?''

''Come on. Give. I want life philosophy. General outlook. Personal anecdotes. Tender memories.''

He dropped his fork, letting it clatter to his plate. ''I thought I was done with finals.''

''You're a tough guy. You can do it.''

''That would assume I had layers. I don't. I'm incredibly superficial. I believe what they print in the newspapers.''

''The *Post* or the *Times?*''

''Ha!''

''Just checking.''

He picked up his fork again. ''So you want a real conversation, eh? I don't know. I'm not good at this.''

''What's to be good at? You talk. I listen. We learn about each other.''

''We've only known each other for an hour. Aren't we supposed to be discussing movies or something?''

She shook her head. ''Too mundane.''

''I like mundane.''

''No, you don't. You like to live life. Not watch it from the sidelines.''

''Touché.''

She studied him for a long moment, during which he took refuge in a large swig of wine. ''Okay,'' she said. ''We'll approach it from another angle. Truth or dare?''

He choked. Put the wineglass down. ''What?''

''You heard me. Truth. Or dare.''

''Megan, are you sure about this?''

''I'm on vacation. The first one I've ever had on my own. I've got a bum leg and a whole week staring at me. I repeat. Truth, or dare?''

3

"OKAY," LUKE SAID. "TRUTH."

"Excellent." She ate for a few minutes, and he could practically see the little wheels and gears spinning inside her head as she chose her question. He should probably be worried, but in fact, her little game was going to make his job much simpler. He hadn't played the game for years, not since high school. But he'd ended up with Jill Pascall's underpants and a hickey the size of a Buick. Pretty good for a freshman.

"What's the dumbest thing you've ever done?

He winced. "Oh, I get it."

"Get what?"

"You're kinky, aren't you? Into humiliation, right?"

"Well, it certainly does get an evening rolling, don't you think?"

"Okay, fine. I'll play. But remember, you're playing, too."

"I'm in," she said, although she had a feeling it was the wine talking, and she'd live to regret this.

"Dumbest thing, huh? I hate to admit it, but I have way too many to choose from. We could be here all night."

"Nope. I don't buy it. Everyone has one spectacularly bad moment. The one that rears its ugly little head when you least expect it. That makes you blush like a nun at an orgy.''

''Nice metaphor.''

''Thanks. Now confess.''

Of course, she was right. He did have one spectacular gaffe in his past, but he wasn't at all sure he wanted to share it. Talk about embarrassment. Jeez. On the other hand, she was going to have to answer the same question, and if he wussed out, so would she. ''Okay, but in years to come, if you should decide to write a tell-all biography about my life, you're not allowed to mention this, got it? This tidbit goes with you to the grave.''

She crossed her heart. ''I swear on pain of death.''

''I can't believe I'm going to actually say this.''

''I can't either. You're drawing it out long enough.''

''Good God, woman, you're brutal.''

She gave him a wicked grin. ''You have no idea.''

He laughed, took another hit of vino, then a deep breath. ''I was thirteen,'' he said, hardly believing he was saying the words. ''I was curious.''

''Ah.''

''Yeah.''

''Go on.''

He cleared his throat. ''I was at my grandmother's club. Where she went swimming. It wasn't a country club or anything fancy like that. More like a senior center. Lots of very old people.''

''Okay.''

''The door to the woman's locker room was open.''

"Oh, no."

"Oh, yes. I repeat. I was thirteen."

She put her hand over her mouth, as if that would hide her laughter. Right.

"So I went inside."

"And?"

"I heard voices. Got scared. So I hid."

"Where?"

"In the laundry bin."

"Oh, God."

"Which would have been fine, if damp. Until the inevitable."

"What?"

"A woman. An old woman, I don't know, she was maybe a hundred, or at least I thought she was, put her towel in the bin. I moved. She pulled my covers, so to speak. She screamed. Damn loud for a woman of her years, let me tell you. They swarmed."

"Oh, God. You must have been mortified."

"You have no idea."

She was laughing now, and his whole face was hot with humiliation.

"They were all naked."

"Oh!"

"And you remember the whole me being thirteen thing, right?"

She nodded, groped for some water.

"So, uh, I was actually, um, involved."

"Involved?"

"Self-involved, if you get my drift."

"Oh, my God."

He nodded, the memory so vivid and painful he

could still smell the chlorine and talcum powder. ''It wasn't exactly my shining moment.''

She tried to speak, but she couldn't. She was laughing too hard. Tears were actually running down her cheeks. It was pretty funny. It hadn't been then, that's for damn sure. But it was now. He chuckled, although his face was still on fire.

After a long time, a really long time, she calmed down enough to speak. ''What happened?''

''Aside from being known as the neighborhood pervert? I was almost arrested. One old lady had heart palpitations. Thank God, I didn't kill anyone. But my grandmother never looked at me the same way again. Needless to say, I was never invited back to the club.''

''I would imagine.''

''Of course, the story got out. My school chums were kind about it, however.''

Megan winced.

''Yeah. Like all thirteen-year-olds. I was called Granny for a long, long time.''

She sniffed, wiped her nose with her napkin. ''I was going to ask why you didn't go to UCLA.''

''Right.''

''Oh, my,'' she said, and then she started giggling again. But this bout was only a few moments. Long enough for him to pour them each more wine, and for him to polish his off.

She lifted her glass to him. ''I salute you, Luke. That is one hell of a tale.''

''Yeah.''

''And you were very brave to tell it.''

''Brave? I can think of another word.''

"No, brave. Wonderfully brave. And I know a lot more about you now, so it worked."

"You know I've been a perv most of my life. I'm not sure that's a good thing. See, I told you we should have talked movies."

"You know that's not true."

"I know nothing of the sort. However, maybe after you tell me your dumbest thing…"

She looked at her watch. "Heavens, I had no idea how late it was. I have to—"

"Not a chance, babe. You're staying right there until I hear it."

She grinned. "Okay. It's only fair. But let's wait till we have dessert, okay? I need sugar courage."

"You didn't let me wait."

"You had wine courage."

"What's the difference?"

"I'll let you know."

Just then, the waiter walked by and Luke caught his attention. Megan ordered crème brûlée, and Luke his chocolate cake. As soon as the waiter left, Luke grinned. "Okay," he said. "Your turn."

Megan knew the dumbest thing she'd ever done. She'd believed her leg didn't matter. She'd believed the accident wouldn't change a thing. She'd even believed Jeff still wanted to marry her. But she wasn't going to confess that to Luke. Even if she hadn't been doing the thing with the cast, she wouldn't. She shuddered just thinking about it.

"You're stalling."

She sipped her coffee, wishing the dessert would get there. "No, I'm not. I'm just waiting for you to play the game correctly."

"Excuse me?"

"You have to play by the rules. You need to ask me if I want truth or dare."

He rolled his eyes. "Fine. Truth or dare?"

Megan smiled. "Dare."

"What!"

She laughed, loving the shock on his gorgeous face. God, was this really happening to her? "You heard me. Dare."

"So you think that's funny, do you?"

She nodded gleefully. Sometimes she just knocked herself out.

"All right, then," he said, lowering his voice to a dangerous pitch. "You want to play it that way? Great. The gloves are off."

Her smile faded. "Wait a minute."

Luke held up a hand. "Nope. You made your decision. You had your chance."

"Come on, Luke…"

"Come on, nothing. You're the one who set up the rules. Now you're going to play by them."

She leaned over and picked up the bottle of wine and poured the rest into her glass. Unfortunately, there was only a sip or two left. She searched the immediate vicinity for the waiter, wondering if she should order the whole bottle of tequila or just a half-dozen shooters.

"I dare you…" Luke said, drawing her gaze with his sotto voce whisper, "…to come up to my room and finish this little game you started."

Megan blinked. She'd thought he was going to dare her to do something awful, like flash the maître d' or sing the national anthem while he paid the check. Going up to his room hadn't crossed her mind.

Instant panic. Her heart went into triple time, her pulse raced, her mouth dried up and she kind of moaned, although maybe it had just been in her head and not out loud.

His laugh seemed to indicate the sound had been audible. Although she failed to see the humor.

"You're the one who chose dare," he said.

She swallowed. Opened her mouth. Then closed it again. "On second thought, truth."

Luke's right brow raised.

"No, wait. You're right. I said dare. I came up with the game. I made you play fair."

"So, you're going to do it? Come with me to my room?"

She studied his eyes for a long moment while she forced herself to take calm, deep breaths. They were the most attractive thing about him, which was saying a lot. She'd been captivated by the color, a dark, deep blue that made her think of oceans and twilight. But more than the color, more than the unfairly long lashes, there was a spark in his eyes, a magic as potent as any spell. Humor, intelligence, honesty, and most important of all, kindness.

That's what she'd tried to capture in her drawing. That odd and fascinating mix of kindness and sensuality. Of wicked élan mixed with humor. She wasn't worried that something bad would happen in his room. In fact, she felt sure it would be something she'd remember for the rest of her life. The scary part was that she liked this Man To Do. Liked him a lot.

And she knew, as clearly as she knew Luke wouldn't hurt her for the world, that if she wasn't wearing the cast, if she was in her brace, with her mangled leg all puny and pathetic, she wouldn't be having this dinner. She wouldn't be playing this game. He wouldn't have even spoken to her.

She didn't blame him. It was just the way it was in the world. Her leg set her apart, made her different. She'd made peace with that.

Only, when she met someone she liked...really liked, it kind of hurt.

"Uh, Megan?"

Uh-oh. She'd been staring. For a long time. "Yes?"

"You don't have to. I'd like you to, but I won't push. I was just, you know, playing."

That, of course, did it. More than anything else he could have said or done, that convinced her to say the hell with her fears and go for it. She just smiled, found the waiter, and asked him to pack their desserts to go. She turned back, unbelievably proud of her courage. She smiled triumphantly at Luke. "I chose dare," she said. "Dare it is."

"Wow."

"You sound surprised."

He grinned. Looked toward the kitchen door. "Think they'd notice if we just left?"

She laughed. "Yeah. I do."

"Damn. See, I've got some brandy up in my room, and there's this fireplace—"

"You have a fireplace?"

He nodded as the waiter came over with the bill and the bag of goodies. Luke grabbed the check, and whipped his credit card into the leather sleeve before she could even protest. "You're gonna love it. I promise."

"Just for the record, you're not an ax-murderer or anything, right?"

He laughed. "Naw. The worst that might happen is me bending your ear about high-tech stocks. You're safe."

She didn't feel safe. In fact, this whole evening had felt risky and unlike her life. Way unlike her life. But, she supposed that was what vacations were for. He'd said he admired people who stepped outside their comfort zone and she wasn't in the same hemisphere as hers.

She grabbed her purse and the crutches and got to her feet with a minimum of wobbling. The cast was still so unfamiliar. Actually, she couldn't decide if it was the cast that was so strange or the absence of her brace. Whatever. Not important. What was important was that she was going to the room of the best-looking man on earth. Or at least the best-looking man here. It was still so hard to believe. She kept wanting to look behind her and see who he was really talking to.

And June said it wouldn't work. Ha!

"Ready?"

"As I'll ever be."

He picked up her pad, which she'd forgotten about, and the desserts, then moved to her side. He smiled, revealing almost perfect white teeth. There was a flaw, however, a crooked front tooth, that somehow made his smile much more charming than if they'd been even. It also made her feel better about her own crooked grin.

They headed for the door. She couldn't help but notice women noticing Luke. Lusting after Luke. She tried not to look too smug. After all, the night was still young, and the possibility of disaster still loomed.

Which was another thing June always clucked at. According to June, optimism was the only way to fly. She was a regular Pollyanna, with visions of sugarplums on the side. Megan leaned the other way… better to be aware of the horrible things that could be lurking around every corner. That way, she'd be a bit prepared if they came about, and pleasantly surprised if they didn't. It was all a matter of perspective.

"This way," he said, touching her lightly at the small of her back.

The shivers he caused felt delicious. Better than the crème brûlée. It had been so long since she'd been touched by a guy. Well, by a guy who wanted to sleep with her. That made all the difference.

She'd shaved her leg, which was a good thing. However, she hadn't really considered the whole taking off her clothes portion of the evening. With the cast, it could be tricky. Oh well. She'd cross that bridge, etc. As long as the lights were off, things couldn't get too out of hand.

The lobby was only slightly less busy than when they'd come in for dinner. The après-ski crowd was out in force, and given the weather and the relative isolation of the resort, it was something of a captive audience. They had a spa, a game room, a large-

screen TV in a sports bar in addition to the eating
establishments, but she'd guess the biggest crowd
was in the big fireplace room. The pickup room.
Maybe everyone was in a Man To Do group online,
who knows?

Luke's hand moved on her back. Not much, just
enough to steer her thoughts away from anything and
anyone else.

"Do you need anything before we go up?" he
asked. "There's the gift shop."

She couldn't think of anything offhand. She'd
come prepared. In her purse were breath mints, lipstick, a brush and three brand-new ribbed "for her
pleasure" condoms. "Nope. I'm good."

"Great." He led her to the elevators, where they
waited in that awkward silence of preboarding, a preview of the even more awkward silence of the actual
elevator ride. She didn't care. She didn't want to talk
to anyone else. She just wanted to get to his room
without tripping.

He was on the eighth floor. She was on four. It
turned out that eight was a lot nicer. The hallway
even had better wall sconces. Instead of the omni-
present antlers, they used an interesting assortment of
twigs, which should have looked tacky, but didn't.
The paintings on the walls were landscapes, but nice
ones. On her floor, there were skiing prints.

"Just down the hall," he said, as they passed the
workout room. She'd thought about checking that
out, and now, she knew where it was. Cool.

At 812, he stopped and used his card key. He held
open the door for her, and she held her breath as she
crossed the threshold. Dare, indeed.

"Brandy?" he asked, as he shut the door behind them.

She nodded. "Wow, this is nice."

"I like it. I've stayed in this room before. It's comfortable."

She walked deeper into the living room. "I'll say." Instead of the utilitarian, nearly generic room she'd rented, his was elegant. A luxury suite, complete with bar, the promised fireplace, a view to die for, and really wonderful furniture. Heavy, sleek and modern, the couch and chairs were burnished leather. The coffee table was pine, as were the end tables. They'd done a great job with accessories, too. Everything from striking modern paintings on the walls to a glass sculpture of an elk that looked like something she'd see in a pricey gallery.

He made it to the bar to put down the dessert bag while she was still giving the place a once-over, and when she found him, he had two snifters on the counter. The brandy was Courvoisier, and even though she knew *bupkis* about liquor, she'd heard that was the good stuff.

"I'm thinking the couch might be more comfortable than a chair," he said. "But you sit where you like."

"Let's give the couch a try," she said, anxious to sit, to let the awful crutches fall. Her armpits hurt, which she wasn't sure was supposed to happen. Perhaps if she'd gone to a real doctor, and gotten prescription crutches—if there were such things—they'd fit better, but beggars, etc.

She hobbled to the couch and maneuvered into place, not plastered to the edge, but not dead center, either. She had a great view of the window and the fireplace, although there was only one thing she really wanted to look at.

The man in question walked toward her, holding the snifters, smiling with a look of anticipation that made her tummy go all wiggy. She needed to remember that look, that sly grin, his arched brow, so she could draw him tomorrow. She wasn't nearly good enough to capture him properly. but she'd give it her all. Hopefully, it would be a nude. And accurate.

"A fire, yes?"

She nodded.

"Don't go anywhere."

"Okay," she said, and she didn't even laugh. It would take an army to get her out of here. Two armies. Which didn't mean she wasn't scared spitless. He'd put the snifters on the coffee table, and she took one, liking the smell as she lifted the glass to her lips. The taste was something else again. Not that the brandy wasn't fabulous in every way, but she wasn't all that fond of booze. She could handle wine, and sometimes she even liked it, but everything else all tended to blur on her uneducated palate. She tended to order shots, which allowed for the least amount of actual tasting to get the desired effect. Brandy wasn't on her short list.

"You like?"

"It's wonderful," she said, meaning him, her, it, so not really lying at all. "Incredible."

He took his own sip as his gaze narrowed, and she felt her cheeks heat. Another sip of brandy, a glance at the fire.

"Truth," he whispered, "or dare?"

"Pardon?"

"Truth or dare?" he repeated, and her cheeks became as hot as the crackling fire.

"It's my turn, isn't it?"

Luke moved around the coffee table and sat down next to her. So close, his knee almost touched hers. Almost. "I don't think so. If I remember correctly, my dare was for you to come up here so we could continue the game. So, technically, it's still my turn. And your dare."

"Interesting interpretation there, Luke. Are you sure you're not a lawyer?"

He grinned. "No, but I used to room with a guy who is. Gave the law some thought, but it wasn't for me. Too much research. But don't change the subject."

"I'm not buying your explanation, roommate or not. It's my turn."

"Okay. Shoot."

She took a deep breath, and let it out, not at all sure if she was ready for the next phase, but what the hell. "Truth or dare?" she asked.

He didn't answer her right away. He sipped more brandy, let his gaze move over her face as if he had all night. She wondered if he was toying with her, or if he really was debating his answer. Of course, she had no clue what she was going to ask him no matter what his response was. Which meant she should be thinking herself, but dammit, how could she when he looked at her like that?

"All right," he said, more to himself than her. "Why not? Let's go for it. I choose dare, Megan."

He leaned slightly toward her, close enough for her to smell the sweet brandy on his breath, feel the pressure of his thigh against her own.

"Dare, huh?"

He nodded.

"Kiss me," she whispered. "I dare you."

"Ah, sweet girl, that's not a dare. That's... inevitable."

4

LUKE SAW HER EYES flutter closed, and her pink lips
part. She offered herself to him, to this strange game,
and yet there was something completely naive and
tender in the gesture. It couldn't be so, but it felt as
if she were offering him her first kiss. Crazy.

He leaned forward that last little inch and gently
licked her lips, letting her get used to the idea of him
while he tasted her for the first time. She was as
sweet as he'd imagined, but softer. If women understood the power of their softness...

One more quick swipe across her pouty lower lip
and he sealed her mouth with his.

Part sigh, part moan, the sound went right to his
cock, and he had to focus on the slow, patient seduction. His hands came up to hold her steady as he
carefully introduced his tongue into her mouth, moving the tip around the inside of her lips. Barely in,
his teeth nibbling delicately at the inner tissue of her
lower lip, he took his time, let the kiss be the goal.
Now he drew her lip in, sucked on it...breathed warm
air into her mouth, then again let his tongue slip between the open lips and back out, taking her a little
deeper each time until he finally pressed his mouth
on Megan's and slowly forced it wide. Still gently,
but breathing harder and with a tighter grip, he

pushed his tongue through the opening. Felt Megan jerk under him and whimper.

His tongue met hers, which had retreated. He wouldn't have that. Not when he was just learning the taste of her, and he sucked her right into his mouth. She made a small, muted, cut-off cry and pulled her tongue back into her own mouth. Surprised, Luke coaxed with little licks and sucks, and finally backed off to murmur, "Hush, Megan. I won't bite."

"Are you sure?"

"I promise," he said. "However, I may nibble."

She giggled as he demonstrated, using the edge of his front teeth on every inch of her upper lip. When he'd finished, she sighed. Acquiesced. And let him draw her in once more.

He pressed against her, just his thigh, but it was enough to feel the heat of her. The kiss went on with no rushing things, without more pressure, more urgency, and yet he felt a coil of tension in his stomach and lower. The trick was to be patient, to wallow in the moment, to make every second the first second and the last.

Megan touched him. His arm, just above the elbow, and he wished he wasn't wearing a sweater. Wished he wasn't wearing anything at all, but then that wasn't part of the plan, was it? Focus, focus and let the momentum build until something had to give.

Pressure, there, higher on his arm, her fingers squeezing him, and then her other hand on his knee. But only for a second. He wanted it back, knew it was only a matter of time.

He forced his concentration back to her lips, to her

taste, and his reward was the soft silk of her mouth
sending pleasure signals to every part of him. Lush,
sweet, ripe, she was his opposite in every way, and
he supposed that's what he craved. Her softness, her
gentle sigh, the tentative licks with the tip of her
tongue. Intrigued, he let up, stilled his assault. She
took over, as he'd hoped, exploring him now with
the same careful rhythm.

As he knew it would, her hand came back to his
knee, and the other moved to his shoulder. She
shifted more toward him and he had to be careful
because of her leg. He didn't want her to be uncomfortable. Hell, he didn't want her feeling anything at
all except what he gave her, what he nurtured.

He felt her nails dig into his thigh and held back
a satisfied grunt. He knew how to play her to get
what he wanted. The real challenge was to see that
she got exactly what she wanted. More, if he did his
job well. Like a particularly tricky mogul run, he had
to know when to ease back, when to go for speed,
just how to maneuver around barriers. He played to
his strengths. His teammates had called him Ice Man,
not because of his love for winter sports but because
he was as stubborn as a glacier, as focused in his
patience as a master jeweler.

Her grip tightened again, and he pulled back. Not
that he wanted to—she was as delectable a woman
as he'd ever known—but if he wanted the ultimate
prize, he couldn't let his whims dictate the course.

He eased away from her, watching as her eyes fluttered open, as she licked her moist lips.

"Well, okay then," she said, struggling for her

own equilibrium. "That was, uh, one heck of a dare."

"I don't believe in half measures," he said, a little surprised at the gruffness in his voice. And the strength of his desire to kiss her again.

"So I guess I won't be daring you to arm wrestle."

He laughed. "I think your dare was a fine choice."

She blinked at him, as if she were adjusting to a bright light. "The last time I played truth or dare, I was in high school. I had to kiss John Foster."

"Oh?"

"John Foster, the boy with the worst breath in Benjamin Franklin High. I think he brushed his teeth once a month, whether he needed to or not."

"So this was better?"

She laughed. "A bit."

"What else did you have to do?"

She picked up her brandy snifter, then leaned back against the couch. If he hadn't been watching for it, he would have missed the slight tremor in her hand. She sounded sure, easy, but there was some shaking going on. He wasn't the only one who wanted more.

"Oh, yeah," she said, and he remembered he'd asked her a question. "I had to drink a shockingly large quantity of cheap wine."

"That doesn't sound good."

"It wasn't. I was sick as a dog all the next day. I told my mother I had the flu, but she didn't believe me. That night I found a pamphlet from the church on my pillow, all about the evils of alcohol and where drinking inevitably led the weak."

"Ah. Did you heed the word?"

She shook her head, making her soft, silky hair

shimmer in the firelight. "Naw. I went on to more and more sordid activities. I actually ditched school once."

"No."

"Yep. It was great, too. My friends and I went to the city. We pulled a Ferris Bueller. Although there was no downtown parade. We did, however, hum 'Twist and Shout' as we went past the civic center."

"Sounds wild."

Megan sighed. "It wasn't. But it was fun. I liked that year a lot."

"You were a senior?"

"Junior."

"I didn't care much for high school," he said. "I concentrated on sports, mostly, although I kept up the grades. I knew if I wanted to go to any kind of a decent college I'd have to get a scholarship."

"That surprises me. I would have guessed you'd loved high school."

"Why?"

"I'll bet you were the star quarterback. Probably the class president. And I'd be willing to put money on you dating the head cheerleader."

"You'd lose."

She sipped her brandy, her fingers toying with the bottom rim of the snifter. "But she was homecoming queen, am I right?"

He grabbed his own drink and took a swig. "Yeah. She was. And to be fair, the only reason she wasn't head cheerleader was because there's never been a more uncoordinated beautiful girl. I swear, it's amazing she didn't kill herself or someone else. Major klutz."

"I imagine you thought it was charming."

"Only to a point. I mean, she couldn't stay up on skis. She tried, I'll give her that, but damn. She couldn't water-ski or roller-blade. She was useless at sports."

Megan's gaze went to her fingers. "I imagine that was tough for you."

"Tough for both of us. She wanted to play, wanted to be part of it all, but she just couldn't."

She looked at him again, and something had shifted, although he couldn't have said what. A light had dimmed somewhere in her eyes. "She was good at other things, though, wasn't she? Maybe sewing or drama or something?"

"She liked scrapbooks. She made them as gifts, kept a ton for herself. They were kind of cool, too."

"Do you know where she is now?"

"No, we lost touch after high school."

"Yeah, that happens."

"So what about you? Cheerleader?"

"God, no. I wasn't part of that crowd."

"What crowd were you in, then?"

"I think back then we were nerds. I'm not sure though. This was in 1995. We might have been dweebs."

He grinned. "I can't picture it."

"No, it's true. I was into drawing, of course, and so I did a lot of work on the school paper and the yearbook. Very unhip."

"But I bet you were good at it, even then. I bet you kicked some high school art ass."

She grinned. "Oh, yeah. That was me, all right. Kung fu artist."

"You really are gifted. I mean, I've only seen the one picture, but damn, it was great. I'm really flattered."

"You caught my eye, what can I say?"

He narrowed his gaze. "Truth, or dare?

She looked worried. "We're still playing?"

"Hell, yes. Come on. Truth or dare?"

"Hmm, I've tried dare. So why don't we go with truth this time."

"Good. I was hoping."

"Why? What evil question are you about to ask?"

"Not evil. But I do expect the absolute truth."

"Uh-oh."

"Why were you drawing me?"

She opened her mouth, but didn't speak. Then she closed it again, took another sip of brandy. "Truth, huh?"

He nodded. "Yep."

Megan's first thought was to demure. At the very least to deflect, but then she thought, why? Why not tell him the absolute truth? What did she have to lose? If she was very lucky, and he liked her answer, maybe he'd kiss her again. The thought made her shiver.

Good God, where had he learned to kiss like that? Talk about a gift. She'd been kissed before, but this was a whole different ball game. It shouldn't even be called kissing. He deserved a whole new word. Something long and intricate that rolled easily on the tongue. Her temperature went up ten degrees just thinking about it.

"Megan?"

"Oh, right." The heat went up another notch at

the thought of him guessing what she'd been thinking. Best to just talk. Tell him what he wanted to know. "I saw you from across the room, and, well, I liked what I saw."

He grinned a bit sheepishly. "Despite what it sounded like, I'm really not fishing. I just wondered why, you know, with a room full of people, you picked me."

"I understand, and I'll do my best to tell you, although honestly, I didn't think about it much at the time. First of all, you have a really excellent behind."

He laughed out loud. "Excellent behind?"

"Yes. Very well-shaped. Don't laugh, it's true. And I'm speaking here as an artist, not a girl."

"Ah, okay. That's different then."

She let him tease her. In fact, she kind of liked it. "Say what you will, but the derriere is an important body part."

"I couldn't agree more."

"Now whose mind is in the gutter?"

He held up his hands. "I never denied it."

She shifted a bit on the couch, trying to make herself more comfortable. It wasn't easy. Her leg, which never was truly pain free, was now far more annoying with the synthetic cast, and a little itchy, to boot. She couldn't scratch, so she'd better distract. "While I appreciated your ass, it wasn't the reason I picked you."

"Damn."

"It was your eyes."

His head went back as if she'd chosen his weakest point. "Really?"

"Of course. You can't tell me you've never been told you have wonderful eyes. I won't believe it."

"I've had a compliment or two, but nothing that I'd write home about."

"Hmm. Odd. Because they really are great. The color alone made me wish I was using paint instead of charcoal. The blue is so deep, it's like looking into midnight."

He got up quickly and headed for the bottle he'd left on the counter. "Okay, enough. I can't do this. It's your turn."

"But I'm not finished."

"Yeah, you are."

"Uncomfortable, are we?"

"Let's change the subject."

He walked back, poured another two fingers into her glass. Then in his own.

"Can I just say one more thing?"

"I don't think so."

"Too bad, I'm going to."

He sighed heavily. "All right. But be quick about it. And don't make me blush."

"Chicken."

He clucked for her. Rather well, actually.

"Okay, I get it. So I'll just say this. You give yourself away with your eyes."

"Huh?"

"It's a good thing. Honest. You don't hide behind them. I saw your humor right away. Your excitement. Your intelligence."

"I don't pay my eyes nearly enough."

"I'm not joking. I can see why you'd be successful at your work. People can trust you."

He sat back down beside her and gave her the most incredulous stare. "Trust me? Did we forget I'm a stockbroker?"

"No, we didn't forget. And I'll bet your clients go along with you far more often than not."

"And you're telling me it's because I tell the truth with my eyes."

"Yes."

He looked at her for a long moment, and the proof was in the pudding. She could see his doubt, his curiosity and his embarrassment. All right there like a printed program. It was rare to find that quality in a grown man. She'd never seen it in anyone past their teens.

"Are we done with this?"

"Yes."

"Thank God. I'm sorry I brought it up."

"Don't be. It's something rare and fine."

He leaned closer to her. "I think you're rare and fine."

"Ah, but would you have said that if I hadn't just complimented the hell out of you?"

He nodded. "Yep."

"Cool."

He smiled, and she watched his mood shift back to where they'd been a few moments ago. He was going to kiss her again. It was right there, plain as day. She hoped he would do it soon. Really soon.

"Your turn," he said.

"Ah. Okay." She touched his leg with the tips of her fingers. "Truth or dare?"

"I liked dare a lot," he said. "Let's do dare."

Her tummy got tight and the shivers returned, but

now she had to figure out what the dare was to be. Another kiss? Or more?

She wanted more. Lots more. But she also didn't want to appear too eager. She hadn't known him for long, but she could already tell he was the kind of man who liked to be in charge. Which was fine, as long as he didn't want anything she wasn't willing to give. In fact, she liked that he was all butch and stuff. Too many of the men she knew were afraid to be macho. Or maybe they just didn't have it in them. She liked macho. To a point, of course. But when it came to seduction, she could be as girly as they came.

Which brought her right back to her dare. If it wasn't a kiss, then what? And what was that wicked little grin about? "I've got it," she said. "I dare you to tell me what you're thinking right this second."

He chuckled. "No problem. I was just thinking about what you'd look like when you came."

She gasped, which made him laugh.

"If you didn't want to hear the answer, you shouldn't have asked the question."

"Point taken," she said.

"But it was what I was thinking."

"I see."

He scooted closer to her, and once again they were touching from knee to hip. She swallowed. Tried to get a few of her brain cells to work. At least she didn't have to wonder where this was all headed.

But, she realized, she wasn't quite as liberal as she'd like to think. Despite the fact that she had come to his room because she wanted to have sex with him, she wasn't prepared to tear off her clothes and shout

"Take me, big boy." Although, to be honest, she did want to end up there. Just not...yet.

"Uh, I think you'd better go next," she said. "And before you have to ask, I'm staying the hell away from dare."

He laughed with that voice of his. Oh, God.

"I don't think truth is going to save you, Megan."

"No?"

He shook his head. "However, the night is young. There are still quite a few things I want to learn about you before I lose the ability to speak coherently."

She sighed. "That's good. Ask away."

"Hmm," he said, touching the edge of her sweater. "What to ask first?"

She held her breath, whether from the anticipation of his question or the way his fingers felt rubbing that tiny spot on her hip, she couldn't say.

"Since this is vacation," he said, "and everyone knows that the rules don't apply while on vacation..."

She breathed. She had to, or pass out.

"...I want you to tell me your wickedest vacation fantasy."

"My what?"

"You know what I mean, Megan. We've all had them. Wild thoughts about what we'd do if there were no consequences. If you knew you weren't ever going to see him again. If all bets were off, and it was just about pure—" he leaned closer "—unadulterated—" his lips brushed her cheek as his warm breath slipped inside her without her permission "—sex."

5

A SOUND CAME OUT OF HER, a cross between a sigh and a squeak, and it pretty much said everything. Pure, unadulterated sex was exactly what she'd signed up for. No consequences was the extra special bonus. And that she'd never see him again made the whole thing possible.

So what was her fantasy? Just being here with Luke was as far as she'd gotten. But what kind of a truth was that?

He wasn't making it easy on her. Not when his lips nuzzled the sensitive skin just below her ear. Hot breath, moist tongue, goose bumps and shivers. Talk about a fantasy.

"Tell me," he whispered, mouthing the word against her flesh. "No censorship allowed. This is fantasy mountain, and you've just won the grand prize.

"I'll say."

He chuckled as he moved his lips to her earlobe. She moaned with delight as he nibbled and nipped, traced the shell of her ear with the pointy tip of his tongue.

"I can't think," she said, groping for something to hold on to. She found his upper thigh and proceeded to squeeze her appreciation.

"Is it soft and sweet?" he asked. "Or wild and hard?"

"Uh-huh."

Again he chuckled, but it wasn't enough to distract her from the sensation of his hand on her sweater. He touched her a few inches below her breast, and she knew he was going to linger there. He was a man who liked it slow, methodical, and that was fine by her. Up to a point.

"Have you dreamed of being tied up?" he asked. "Unable to move as your body is ravished from head to toe?"

"Uh, I don't think so."

"Oh, you'd remember," he said. "But maybe that's not your thing. Maybe you like to be on top. In control."

"I don't know. You're doing a pretty good job here."

He growled, then moved his lips to her temple. He licked her skin right there, the flat of his tongue in a long, slow swipe that caused a maelstrom inside her. "Oh, God. That's..."

"You like that?"

"Uh-huh."

"That's nothing. That's an hors d'oeuvre. The main course is going to make you crazy."

"Too late."

The hand on her tummy rubbed in slow circles and the edge of his fingers brushed the underside of her breast. She had to force herself to stay still. Well, relatively still. She couldn't have stopped trembling if her life depended on it. But she didn't grab his hand and put it forcibly on her breast, and that was triumph of will.

"I can think of a lot of things I'd like to do with you, Megan," he said. "Of course, your leg in the cast presents an interesting challenge."

"Interesting?"

"Very. Of course, the old standby missionary would work just fine, but that's not enough. Not nearly enough."

"No?"

"Uh-uh. For you, I'd have to think about it. Come up with a plan. Several plans. Every plan."

She let go a breath she hadn't realized she'd held. "Go on."

"You, sitting on the edge of the bed. Legs spread and comfortable."

She'd meant his hand, but this was good. This was very good.

"Me, on the floor. Doing all the work. Taking you way the hell past where you think you can go."

The sound came again, that moany squeak thing. Because she could picture it. Picture him. His magical tongue driving her wild. Holding on to the edge of the bed for dear life. She squirmed, but that only made things worse.

Mercifully, he finally moved his hand that last inch, and he cupped her breast. She knew he had to feel the hard point of her nipple. He squeezed very gently, and she pushed herself against him. And because he clearly thought it was his job to make her insane, he pulled back so the pressure didn't increase an iota.

"Bastard," she whispered.

"Oh, yes," he said. "I am. You'll be cursing me a lot tonight. But in the end, you'll thank me."

"Too bad you don't have any confidence in yourself, Luke. You might want to work on that."

He laughed. Then his lips covered hers and his tongue plunged inside her mouth, and she was right there on the edge of an orgasm. He hadn't even touched her down there, but it didn't seem to matter. She squeezed her legs together, rubbed against the couch, desperate to go the distance. So close… almost…

He finally squeezed her breast, rubbed against her nipple while his tongue went in and out of her mouth in a preview of what was to come.

She couldn't stand it. She moved her own hand down to the juncture of her thighs and pressed against her mound.

Her muscles tightened, she stopped breathing and all her concentration focused on crossing over, on coming, and she was almost there, almost—

He grabbed her wrist and pulled it away.

Held her tight.

She struggled, but he didn't give an inch.

He laughed, shook his head. "Uh-uh. Not yet, my dear." Then he kissed her again, not letting her touch herself at all.

She moaned, tried once more to break free, but he didn't let her. He did pull back. Far enough back that she could look into his eyes. Watch him shake his head slowly from side to side.

"You didn't finish," he said.

"I know!" She stared hard at his iron grip on her wrist.

"That's not what I meant. You called truth. But you didn't tell me your fantasy."

"You were doing a great job. I felt redundant."

He laughed again. God, she was liking that sound, even when he was being so terribly cruel.

"I want to hear you say it. All of it. And I want details."

"Or?"

He glanced down. "I'm afraid I won't get my dare. Sad, too, because I think you'd be beautiful when you orgasm. Yep, it would be a damn shame."

"I had no idea."

"What?"

"That you could be so mean."

"It's your game. I'm just making sure it's played correctly."

"I don't seem to recall the 'no orgasm' rule. Is that in Hoyle?"

"If it isn't, it should be."

"So you're not going to let up?"

"Sorry. Truly I am."

"Oh, well. It was fun. But it's late, and I'm kind of tired...."

His eyes widened in shock, and even though she should have carried out the threat, she couldn't. She laughed. Kissed him on the lips. "You want to hear my fantasy?"

He nodded.

"Fine. But first, let go."

"Can I trust you?"

"You'll have to find that out."

"All right. But only because I'm a really nice guy."

"Ha!"

He let go of her wrist, and she took one last deep breath. Talk about jumping in the deep end. She was going for it. All the way. Bold as brass. She wasn't Megan tonight. Not even close. She was a femme fatale, a siren, a vamp. And she was going to enjoy every second of it.

She leaned in close to him and put her mouth right up to his ear. "It starts with a kiss," she whispered. "Long, slow, deep. The kind of kiss that starts brush fires. Kisses you do so very well."

His hand went once more to her breast, but it was her turn to hold him steady, and not let him touch. "Patience, Luke. Isn't that your forte?"

He grunted, and she knew she'd nailed him. He wanted patience. Let him get through this.

She licked his ear, mimicking his actions. She hesitated, but then remembered. *No consequences.* No holds barred.

"Then you take my clothes off. One thing at a time. And as you peel away the material, you kiss each part of me that's revealed.

"First, the curve of my shoulder. Then the hollow of my neck. You can smell my perfume, can't you? It's called 'Sinful,' and I put some on tonight, just for you.

"Then you slip off my bra."

He pulled at his hand, but she'd been prepared for that. He wasn't going to get free. Not till she was good and ready. However, she did shift on the couch, freeing her other hand to wander anywhere her little heart desired.

"Payback's a bitch, isn't it, Luke."

He turned his head, tried to kiss her, but she didn't let him. This was her show now, and she was going to give as good as she'd gotten.

She waited patiently until he got back in position, and when her lips were just brushing his ear, she went on. "You see my hard, aching nipples. The soft curve of my breasts. You touch them, feel the soft skin, the warmth. You feel my heartbeat. And then you take that talented tongue and you taste the tip of my nipple, making it ache for your mouth. You suck it inside, pulling at the hard bud until I'm squirming from the pleasure."

He did his own little squirm for her and she leaned back a few inches so she could see the front of his pants. Okay then, he was paying attention.

She smiled as she leaned into him, as she laid her free hand on his thigh. "You take your time with both breasts, using your lips, your tongue, your teeth. I'm so ready for you."

She moved her hand, circling his leg as he'd circled her tummy.

"And then you take off my pants. I'm wearing white lace panties. Tiny little panties that have no back to speak off. Damp little panties. But first, you kiss my tummy, tickle my belly button. Rub your cheek against my skin.

"Can you see it, Luke? Can you picture your mouth right—" she nipped his earlobe "—there?"

He moaned, jerked his hand and almost got away.

"Uh, uh, uh. You wanted my fantasy. You're going to be a good boy and wait till I'm all finished."

"It's a dumb game," he said. "It isn't even in Hoyle's."

"It should be. And if we do this really well, maybe we'll make it into another book. Perhaps Guinness."

"What, for the longest period of extended fore-play?"

"Sure, why not? Let's go for it."

"If I promise to be very, very good, can we jump to the finale?"

"Not a chance."

"Damn."

"Shall I go on?"

"No. Don't. Stop now. Let me—"

"I stop now and I go to my room."

He turned her head sharply, so he could look into her eyes. "Can I come?"

"Not until I let you."

"You do realize I'll get you back for this."

"Promises, promises."

"You're asking for it, lady."

"Let's see, now. Where was I?"

"Your panties. The white ones."

"Ah, yes. But before we take those off, you have a lot of exploring to do."

"Exploring," he repeated, only his voice was more tense.

"The curve of my hip bone. The soft spot at the top of my thigh. You know those places, don't you? So soft. Pale. You feel me trembling beneath you as you lick and suck."

He whined, and she loved it.

"Then you take the edge of my white, tiny panties between your teeth, and you tug them down, down—"

"Oh, God."

"I spread my legs, lift up, so they pull free, and that's when you see how moist and swollen I am. How ready."

"Please, Megan," he begged. "I can do this. I'd be really good at this."

"I'll bet you would be."

"It would be a lot more fun than we're having now."

"You're not having fun?"

"I'm in pain. How can that be fun?"

"Oh, I think you'll live."

"I won't. And it'll be your fault."

"I'll take the blame."

"Dammit, don't take anything. Just hurry."

"Hurry? I can't believe you said that. You haven't rushed a thing so far."

"Right. But I would have if you'd just given me a few more minutes."

"Luke, I think your nose just got bigger."

"Honey, that's not my nose."

She laughed. "You are too cute."

"Your legs were spread. Your ass in the air."

"Okay, okay." She moved her hand up, hovered right next to the bulge in his pants but she didn't quite touch any of the good parts.

"Once my panties are gone, you move between my thighs. You spread me open and touch my lips with the tips of your fingers. Petting me, like a pussy cat. Making me purr."

"Oh, shit."

"Shh," she said. "Close your eyes. Picture it. I'm open, wet, ready for anything. You've promised me kisses. And kisses are just the beginning."

"Megan."

"Yes?"

"What can I say to make you stop this torture?"

"Bribery? Is that what you're talking about?"

"Sure. Why not. Take anything. My apartment. My life savings."

"Oh, Luke, you don't mean that."

"Don't count on it."

She laughed, loving the power, but in truth, he wasn't the only one anxious to move from theory to practice. Time to up the stakes.

"I'll tell you what," she said. "I'll hurry, if you promise not to move. Not a muscle. Okay?"

"And you called me mean?"

"Is it a deal?"

"Yeah, okay. Only, Megan?"

"Yes?"

"I'm begging now."

"Got it." She let him go, and a second later she cupped his erection, and for a moment, she had to pause to appreciate it. Oh, my, this was one gifted guy. One very hard gifted guy.

"You put a pillow under me," she said, her eyes closing as she rubbed him, squeezed her own legs together. "And I'm open to whatever you want to do to me. You lean down and run your tongue all the way up my lips. You taste me, and…"

"What?"

"Um, Luke?"

"Yes?"

"Screw it. This is my fantasy. Right here. Right now. Only, we have way too many clothes on, don't you think?"

He jerked his head around to look at her, and the desperation in his eyes made her laugh.

"Don't tease," he said. "It's not nice."

"I'm not teasing. I'm waiting."

"Oh, God."

"Truth or dare, Luke?"

"Dare. Truth. Anything. Everything."

"No, come on. Pick."

He turned on the couch, grabbed her by the shoulders and pushed her back. "I pick you," he said. Then he kissed her, and kissed her hard.

6

LUKE MIGHT NOT be a genius, but he could take a hint. The woman was ready, and Jesus, so was he. In fact, he had to focus right now on something, anything, that wasn't his cock.

Getting Megan naked would do. She'd already started the process by lifting her sweater, and while part of him wanted to savor the moment of first seeing her, other, more demanding parts had him reaching for her pants.

By the time he had her zipper down, her sweater was on the floor, and he took a quick second to admire her pretty white bra. Damn, he loved them like that. Nothing too ornate, but feminine and lacy. She didn't seem all that anxious to keep it on, and he went back to his task. She'd cut her pant leg so that it just covered the top of her cast, so it wasn't all that difficult to remove them, but he had to be gentle, and that wasn't so easy. If she hadn't had the broken leg, he'd have gotten caveman on her and ripped the damn things off, but as it was, he just moved as efficiently as he could until he'd gotten them down her legs, taken off her shoes, and finished removing the pants. He dropped them in the vicinity of her sweater and bra, forgetting about them and everything else as he saw that she was, indeed, wearing tiny white pant-

ies with no back to speak of. He hadn't thought he
could get harder. He'd been wrong.

"I need some help here," she said, and he woke
up from his hormone-induced haze. She was attempt-
ing to scoot herself over on the couch so that she
could lay back, but he nixed that plan. Not enough
room. Unfortunately, there wasn't a fur rug laid out
in front of the fireplace, and the carpet looked uncomfortable. Lucky for him, the suite came with a
bed.

He stood up, the pressure in his slacks uncomfortable as hell, and scooped Megan into his arms. She
cried out and he froze. "You okay?"

She nodded. "Fine. Surprised, but fine."

"Great." He kissed her, once, hard on the lips,
then headed for the bedroom. On the way, he got to
spend some quality time staring at her breasts. They
weren't too big, but not too small, either. He'd guess
a C-cup, but maybe a B. It didn't matter. They were
incredible. Round, pert, with sharp nipples that
begged to be sucked. He needed more hands. Or to
put her down.

He kicked open the door and walked over to the
king-size bed. The maid had turned down the sheets,
and that made things easier. He put Megan down
carefully, sitting her up on the edge of the bed, then
yanked the rest of the bedclothes down so she could
be covered if she wanted to. Personally, he didn't
want any part of her hidden, but it probably wasn't
really that hot in the room.

"You okay?" he asked again.

She nodded.

He grinned, then set the land speed record for undressing. There was a tense moment when he took off his shoes, but he didn't fall. Sliding his European boxers down was a relief, as they'd gotten so damn tight. His erection, once freed, slapped his stomach, leaving a drop of clear fluid just below his belly button.

Megan whistled, and his smile broadened. He'd hoped she wouldn't be disappointed, and it sounded like he didn't have to worry.

He debated his next move. Get down on his knees and taste her, like she'd described? Or lay her back and take her deep, hard and fast?

She made the decision for him by taking his hand, pulling him to the bed as she lay back. Deep, hard and fast it was.

"Oh, God, Megan."

"I know," she whispered. "But I need you to lift my leg up."

He did, forcing himself to move carefully and not toss her leg around. Once she was settled back, her head on the pillow, he climbed next to her. "You look amazing," he said. "So beautiful."

She smiled, touched his cheek with her hand, and then he couldn't wait another second. He kissed her.

She moaned into his mouth as he got himself positioned for maximum access. Her tongue dipped inside him and it was his turn to groan. He reached down, touching the edge of her panties. A second later, he found out she'd been telling the truth about being so damp. So ready.

He slipped his fingers underneath the wisp of white silk, and found the softest place on earth. The inside of a woman's pussy had no equal. Nothing came close to the velvety heat. He hated the fact that he'd have to use a condom, but before that moment came, he wanted to feel her, touch her, learn the terrain. He would make her come tonight, make her cry out, scratch his back, pray for mercy. He'd make this a fantasy night for both of them.

He deepened his kiss, and found her clit with his index finger. It was already swollen, ripe, and he rubbed it in gentle circles, slowly, slowly applying more pressure as he quickened his pace.

She gasped, squirmed beneath him. He'd always been a better reactor than actor, taking his cues from his partner. And Megan was incredibly responsive. He kept rubbing, kept plunging his tongue inside her, listening to her moans, her cries. Her muscles began the dance, tensing up as she started the climb to climax. He moved his leg on top of her thigh so he could feel it when it happened, not just with his fingers but with his body.

He was going to get his dare, any second now, and he wanted to see her face. He pulled back from the kiss and was rewarded with her total abandon. Her dark hair wild on the white pillowcase, her eyes shut tight, her face a mask of concentration and her feral gasps and moans making him crazy to bury himself deep inside her.

She grabbed the sheet with one fist, his arm with her other, and every muscle in her body strained. She made no noise at all and that was his cue. Like a virtuoso playing the violin, he rubbed her clit with one finger, vibrating her until she came with an explosive spasm. She cried out, dug her nails into his flesh, pulled the sheet free from the corner, clamped his hand between her thighs, and she stayed in that space for second after second, keening her pleasure until with a snap, she moved away from the pressure he'd eased, but hadn't released.

There was just enough time now to grab a condom from the nightstand, rip it open and unfurl the latex over his cock. She was still trembling as he spread her legs, pushed the one back, put himself in position.

She was still in the afterglow of her orgasm when he thrust himself inside her, all the way to the hilt in one, hard, fast push.

She cried out so loudly he figured they'd be getting a call from the front desk, but he didn't give a damn. He was in her, sheathed in the hottest, softest, safest place in the world, and she squeezed him as he moved in, out, the friction unbearable, the sensation too much to be able to hold off for long.

"Megan," he whispered between gritted teeth.

She answered him with an inarticulate moan.

"Come for me, baby. One more time."

"Oh, God. I can't…"

She squeezed him tighter with her internal muscles, and that was it. He felt the rush all the way from his toes until he slammed into her, and exploded like a roman candle.

He heard his own voice from somewhere in the distance, heard her cry out once more. Felt her spasms match his own, squeezing, releasing…

He collapsed, careful not to land too hard on top of her, but unable to gather enough strength to get clear. It was fine, actually, as he was able to curl around her, put his hand on her breast, feel her heart pounding and her chest rise and fall. He closed his eyes, and tried to remember how to breathe.

MEGAN LISTENED to the echo of her heartbeat as she lay snuggled against Luke. His breathing was as rapid as hers, which surprised her a little. He was in such good shape, she'd have figured he wouldn't be out of breath climbing Everest.

On the other hand, it had been breathtaking. Holy shit, she'd never… She'd read about sex like that, and there'd always been a part of her that while wishing it were so, knew that it was all purple prose and big talk. The sad truth about sex had never bothered her. She was more interested in intimacy than athletics, anyway. At least she had been until about ten minutes ago. No wonder wars were fought over sex! So much made sense now. Poetry. One-night stands. Affairs.

Boy, did she pick the right Man To Do. She giggled.

He squeezed her waist. "What's so funny?"

"Nothing. Just an odd thought."

"Ah."

"Are you coherent?"

"I think so. But I won't be operating any heavy machinery for awhile."

"That was…" She searched for words, but no adjective seemed strong enough.

"No kidding."

"I hope this isn't too personal, but is it always like that for you?"

He laughed. "No. Oh, man, no. Which is a good thing because I'd probably starve to death. I wouldn't want to do anything as mundane as eating or sleeping. It would wreak havoc on the master plan.''

"Oh, okay, then.''

"What about you?''

"No, it's not always like that for me. In fact, it's never been like that for me.''

"Seriously?''

"I'm too exhausted to lie.''

"Well, cool.''

She smiled. He sounded like a kid. A really stunning kid.

"In a second, I'm going to pull up the blankets,'' he said. "I promise.''

"Take your time.''

He relaxed against her, his head nestling in the crook of her shoulder. "Okay.''

"Luke?''

"Hmm?''

"What's the master plan?''

"What?''

"You said it would wreak havoc on the master plan.''

"The master plan,'' he said, "is for me to work my ass off for the next eight or so years, amass enough capital to live off the interest, then retire at forty. Forty-five on the outside.''

"Wow, you really must be a good stockbroker.''

"I'm not too shabby.''

"Any hot tips for me?''

"Yeah. Sure. When my brain starts functioning again, I'll tell you what I can.''

"Good, because I want to start my own line of clothing. Being filthy rich would help.''

"No sweat."

"Luke?"

"Hmm?"

"I think I need those covers now."

He didn't say anything for a moment, but he did lift his head. She would have gotten the covers herself, but with him lying on her, and her cast and all...

"Right," he said, then he was sitting up and a moment later she was covered. To her delight, he got right back into position, all curled around her, making her feel quite delicious.

All because of a cast. A little duplicity, some camouflage, and here she was—ridden hard and put away wet by the most gorgeous guy on the mountain.

The thought made her smile, but not for long. Images of her real life intruded. The look she got when someone new saw her leg. Curiosity first, then the relief that it was her, not them, followed immediately by dismissal. In two hot seconds she transformed from woman, potential mate or friend, to cripple, and there wasn't a damn thing she could do about it.

Yeah, okay, if they talked, if circumstances led them into conversation, she came back into personhood. She filled in as time went on and became an individual, but the crippled part never really went away.

June was different. And so were a couple of her other friends, but for the most part, it was the way it was.

Dammit, she deserved this night. She only wished...

Better nip that thought in the bud. If wishes were horses, et cetera. She should just be grateful for small favors, and let it go.

Luke's breath had evened and slowed. In fact, she was sure he was sleeping. Which was a smart thing to do. She should follow suit.

And she would. Soon. But first, she was going to memorize the way his leg felt draped over her. The feel of his hard chest against her back. She was going to remember this night for years to come, and she wanted to get it right.

7

LUKE WOKE UP to sunlight and the feel of a woman. Soft flesh under his hand, against his chest. The memory of last night came back, and his morning hard-on got even harder.

He had no idea why the sex had been so hot, and frankly, he didn't care. Maybe it was the game, the teasing. Maybe it was because he liked talking to her. Then again, perhaps it had been a fluke.

Only one way to find out.

He grinned as he cupped her breast. He rubbed her softly, wanting her to wake up in the right mood. Something told him she wouldn't object to his priming the pump, so to speak.

Her nipple swelled nicely beneath his palm. He shifted so that his other hand was free to explore her hip, the flat plane of her tummy, the soft curls at the juncture of her thighs.

She moaned quietly as his fingers dipped inside her, as he gently rubbed her clitoris. Even better, she wiggled against him, capturing his cock in a warm squeeze play between her behind and his belly.

He kissed her shoulder, then the space beneath her ear where she smelled like roses and vanilla.

Closing his eyes, he relaxed, prepared to take as

much time as needed to wake her properly. As it turned out, the wait wasn't long at all.

He felt her hand on his arm, and then she reached back between them, easing forward so she could grip his cock.

He hissed with the intense pleasure of her touch, and as she rubbed him, he returned the favor, concentrating on giving her a morning orgasm that would make her forget about the night before.

"Oh, my," she whispered.

He smiled, nibbled on her earlobe.

"This is a very nice way to wake up," she said, rubbing her index finger on the sensitive spot below his glans. "It beats the heck out of an alarm clock."

"Glad to make your morning special."

She sighed, and he upped the pace. He wanted her to come first, and given his reaction to her ministrations, he needed to work fast. No way he was going to hold off for long.

He rubbed her harder, making her squirm nicely. Her breathing accelerated, and he felt the telltale muscle tension in her legs and back.

He kept a steady rhythm until she let go of him. Then he went for it.

She gasped, arched and spasmed, her chest and neck flushed and her eyes tightly closed. He let her ride the wave, then he grabbed another condom and whipped that puppy on as fast as he could, because damn, he was ready.

He curled against her again, both of them on their sides so she wouldn't have to move her bad leg. He shifted her legs so he had access to her sweet spot, then eased himself inside her.

She squeezed him with her internal muscles, her low moan making him grit his teeth. When he was all the way in her, he paused. He wanted this to last, although he had his doubts about his chances for success.

His muscles tensed as he rocked back and forth, sliding into her creamy depth, then pulling almost all the way out.

He thought of his portfolio, seeing the stock symbols scroll past his mind's eye, but the distraction didn't work. After a few moments, he gave it up completely. The orgasm ship had set sail and there was no turning back.

He gripped her with his arm, lifted her good leg higher, and then there was nothing in the universe except his cock and her pussy.

He cried out as he came, the release so intense it was close to pain. It took a long time for him to empty, and even after, when she did that little Kegel maneuver, he spasmed inside her.

"Ask me," she said,

"What?"

"You know."

He didn't. Not for awhile at least. Then he understood. "Truth or dare?"

"Truth."

"Okay. Truth. What are you feeling right now?"

"Wrung out. Happy. A little achy. Did I say happy?"

He chuckled. "You certainly did."

"Okay, then."

He kissed her shoulder again. "I'll tell you the

truth, too. I've had one hell of a good time with you. It's been fantastic.''

She reached back, found his hand and squeezed it. "Thanks."

"No, no. It was entirely my pleasure."

"Not entirely."

"I didn't want to presume."

"I'll tell you a secret. I'm lousy at faking it. I mean it. I can't fake it to save my life."

"Really? That's rare."

"I know. And there were a couple of times in my life when faking it would have been far preferable."

"I don't get it. You're so responsive I would think anyone worth his salt could make you, uh, happy."

"I think it's a question of the right stimuli."

"Hmm, I like the sound of that."

"Speaking of stimuli," she said, shifting her butt. "I need to go to the bathroom."

"Understood." He rolled back, got up and walked around to her side of the bed. "Mademoiselle," he said, holding out his hand.

She grinned as she took hold of him. It always amazed her about men being naked. Not a one she'd met gave a damn, and pranced about in the altogether whenever the opportunity arose. Unlike her and all her women friends who headed for cover the moment the lights were on. At least with Luke, it was a treat. A virtual eye festival, complete with a hot dog and balloons. She giggled at the image as she sat up. Her leg felt stiff and clumsy, and she wished she could take off the cast. Wished, for one shimmering moment, that Luke wouldn't care. But that was foolish.

"Hold tight," he said, then he went into the living room.

She gathered the sheet from the bed, pulling it free, then wrapping it around her, toga style.

Luke got her crutches from their perch against the couch, then gathered her clothes and his. He smiled as he thought about their conversation last night. Megan had surprised him, which hadn't happened in a while. If things were different, he'd like to have her as a friend. But his experience over the past few years had made it clear that being friends with a woman was only possible if there was no sex. And there was no way in hell he would be able to see Megan and not want her.

He went back to the bedroom. She was still sitting on the edge of the bed, but she'd covered herself up in a sheet. Too bad. He liked looking at her. On the other hand, it was probably for the best. He needed to get out on the slopes, and if he wasn't careful, he'd end up staying in bed all day.

He paused for a moment, wondering if he should do that very thing, but no. He only had a few days left of his vacation, and the plan was to get in as much time as possible on skis. Besides, spending much more time with Megan wasn't smart. She was great, no question about that, but there were many other fine, beautiful women to get to know before he went back home.

She was on her feet, adjusting her impromptu toga. "You might want to hit the john before I do," she said. "I'm not exactly speedy with this stupid cast."

"Ah, thanks." He kissed her on the cheek. "I'll hurry."

"I'd appreciate it."

Luke headed to the bathroom, his focus already shifting to his first run. He had the new skis to try, and he wanted to check the binding on his boots. He closed the door and left Megan behind.

MEGAN REFUSED to be bummed. She'd known from the get-go that Luke was a one-night stand. She'd walked into the situation with her eyes wide-open. She'd had her Man To Do, and he'd been spectacular. Who knows, maybe she'd even meet someone else. She couldn't imagine having a better time but hey, she'd never imagined herself with someone like Luke.

She pulled her hair back into a ponytail, checked to make sure her mascara wasn't all over her cheeks, then adjusted her sweater before she got her crutches.

She'd shower in her room. The cast Darlene had put on was synthetic which meant she could get it wet, but she still wanted to be careful. She'd brought plastic to wrap it in, mostly because she'd been warned about the itching factor. It was a small price to pay for the freedom the cast afforded.

Damn, but she liked being normal.

When she walked into Luke's bedroom, he was already dressed in his ski clothes. Black pants, maroon sweater, black jacket. He looked good enough to eat.

"You ready?" he asked.

She nodded. "Yep."

"Great." He picked up his ski equipment as they walked through the living room, then held the door open for her. "What are you going to do all day?"

"Sleep, draw, eat, then maybe sleep some more."

"Sounds great."

"Not as great as skiing."

"True."

"It's okay. I'm sure I'll find many ways to amuse myself."

"I bet you will." He closed the door then walked beside her to the elevator. He smiled at her, and for the first time since they'd met, she felt awkward. Nothing sucked more than the morning after. Not that she'd experienced so many of them, but it was never pleasant. Mostly, though, she was left in her apartment, with the scent of sex clinging to the sheets. This was the first time she'd left a hotel room.

The silence ended with the ding of the elevator bell. They got in, and she pressed the button for her floor. They rode down in silence, and she wished there was a way to tell him what a wonderful time she'd had without making him nervous. When they reached her floor, she pasted on her most casual smile. "Thanks again, Luke. It was really fun."

"Truth?" he said, holding the door open.

She nodded.

"You're something special." He kissed her cheek, then her lips. "I can't remember when I've had a better night."

"Same here," she said. "Now go ski. I'd tell you to break a leg, but I wouldn't recommend it."

His smile was so warm it made her forget for a second that whatever they had been to each other was officially over. Then she stepped into the hallway, and the truth came to rest as he waved goodbye. She was alone. Literally and figuratively. But she had a really great memory, right? A whole night she could think about whenever she wanted.

Now, however, she was going to bathe. Then she'd pull out her laptop and report in to Eve's Apple. Boy, the girls were going to be green with envy.

GET YOUR BEVERAGE of choice and settle in, girlfriends. I've got a tale to tell.

Megan took a moment to sip her own coffee. The shower portion of the morning had taken far less time than she'd feared, as the plastic on her leg was easily affixed with the large rubber bands she'd brought from home. She'd put on her snuggly old pink chenille robe, wrapped her hair turban-style in a towel and made the in-room coffee, wishing she had some nice hazelnut cream to put in it. She'd piled pillows against the headboard and settled on the bed, her bum leg stretched out before her like a white stump. Never mind. The cast might be ungainly and it might itch, but it had done the trick.

The last time I wrote, she typed, *I told you guys about the cast, and how it felt. What I didn't say was that I was scared to death. What if it didn't matter? What if all the trouble I have meeting guys isn't my leg at all, but* me? *It wasn't easy admitting how I feel, especially because I'm not supposed to feel this way. I'm supposed to be mature, and confident, and wear my brace like a Gucci scarf, dismissing those who find it odd or uncomfortable without so much as a by-your-leave.*

The truth is, I don't feel that, I'm not terribly mature about it and dammit, for once in my life I'm going to be right out front with it. Having my leg crushed sucked. It was horrible and painful and it changed everything. Aside from Jeff's disappearing act, losing my mom and having to be in that damn wheelchair for so long, it's just plain ugly. And even if I wear long skirts or pants, I know that if I meet some guy, and he doesn't seem to care about my limp or my brace, I know that if things get serious at all, I'll need to get naked at some point, and then what?

It must be like a guy having a really, really tiny dick, you know? No matter what, he's got to deal with it, and he's got to find that rare woman who truly doesn't care. The operative word there being rare. In my experience, people are a hell of a lot more shallow than I even care to think about. Including me. It's true. I'm as shallow as the next person, even though I try not to be. I try to see the inner beauty in everyone, honest. But does that mean I can't appreciate outer beauty once in a while?

Oh, sorry. Got off on a little tangent there. Where was I? Oh, yeah. Wondering if I'm incredibly paranoid about my leg and it truly makes no difference to a living soul, and therefore, wondering if all my problems stem from the fact that I'm hopelessly dull, unattractive and have bad breath. Well, I don't have to worry about that. Why, you ask? Because, my beauties, I met my Man To Do my first night out!

She grinned with satisfaction. June would be eating some major crow, that's for sure.

His name is Luke, and—warning: Shallow alert— he's so unbelievably gorgeous that at first I thought he might be a model or an actor. Turns out he's a stockbroker in Manhattan, and a successful one, if his suite was any indication.

Aha. I can tell you all raised your collective brows. Yes, I saw his suite. But you'll have to wait to hear that part. First, there was the meet. I had ensconced myself in the main lobby area, the central meeting place for the après-ski crowd, and I had my trusty pad on my knees, sketching this and that, when I saw him. My first glimpse was of his ass, and let me just say this...there is a God, and she's a woman. <g> When I finally got around to looking at his face, I was even more dazzled. Dark hair, stunning, dark blue eyes, great smile with perfect not-too-thick-not- too-thin lips. Cheekbones to die for, and oh, my God, his shoulders! I know that's not his face. His face, especially when he laughed, was the visage dreams are made of. I had to draw him. I got so involved with said sketch that I didn't notice he was standing behind me until he spoke! He liked the drawing, was flattered and sat himself down on the ottoman along- side my cast. We chatted. I neither drooled nor burped or did anything else in the body-function hu- miliation package. I even managed to carry on a pretty decent conversation. So decent, it turns out, that he invited me to dine with him. In the good res- taurant.

Fast forward to dinner. Yummy food, even yummier conversation. But wait...it gets better. Somehow, we ended up playing truth or dare. It was too cool, and way naughty, and dinner ended with a dare to go back to his room.

Megan gave herself a moment. She sipped more coffee, closed her eyes, leaned her head back. All the while remembering each step with him, snippets of conversation, the way his hand felt on the small of her back. It was like taking a warm bath on a cold night, immersing herself in the purely hedonistic pleasure of a night with no consequences. A night where she could be whoever the hell she wanted. She sighed as she adjusted the laptop.

Here comes the suite part. He opened a bottle of brandy, a really expensive bottle, and we drank by the fireplace. Things led to things, truths led to dares, and then we were kissing and touching and taking off clothes…. I won't go into detail, but he carried me *to the bedroom, and we made love. It was, without hesitation or doubt, the most intense, fabulous, exciting night I've ever had. He wasn't just gorgeous, but talented, too! I mean, kids, the heavens parted, the angels wept. I fell asleep from pure exhaustion.*

I wish to publicly thank the originators of the fine, brilliant Man To Do *concept, and as soon as I figure out how, I intend to submit their names to the Nobel committee.*

And what did I say about the leg? It was nothing. I mean, we had to get creative about positions and stuff, but it wasn't an issue. Just like I'd hoped. Better. I was a real girl (Pinocchio, anyone?) for the whole night. What a rush.

She sighed. It had been a rush. But it was also over, and that part wasn't so much fun. Oh, well. That's what MTD was all about. It wasn't Man To Fall In Love With.

And now, I have five days ahead of me during which I plan to have a massage, eat many gooey desserts, sleep late, flirt as if I'm the hottest thing walking—even on crutches—and drink, quite possibly to excess. This is my vacation *don't you know, and I intend to* vacate. *Uh, wait, that isn't quite what I mean. Oh, the heck with it.*

Now, I want to hear how—

A knock on the door startled her, and she almost spilled her coffee. It was undoubtedly the maid, but Megan wanted her to come back later. "Hold on," she said as she maneuvered herself into a standing position, crutches in place. "I'm coming."

She got to the door, and after a slight fumble, got it open. Only it wasn't the maid.

It was Luke.

"Hey," he said.

"Hey, back."

"I, uh, just wanted to tell you that I'm going to be on the Big Ben slope today. You can see it from the outdoor café."

His face had been a little pink when she'd opened the door and had grown considerably redder with each word.

"I just thought if, well, if you were there at about one-thirty, maybe we could hook up for, uh, lunch."

She was glad she had the crutches under her pits, or she would have crumpled to the floor. Nothing could have surprised her more. He'd been so... done...this morning. Over and out. Finito. And yet, here he was.

"But if you have other plans—"

"No!" She swallowed, breathed. Promised herself not to yell again. "I'd like that. I have to eat anyway, and that patio is great for people watching." She stopped. Saying more would only lead to foot-in-mouth.

"Great. Okay, then," he said, still blushing like a virgin. "I'll see you."

"Okay."

"Yeah." He leaned forward, then stopped. Leaned in again, and this time, he kissed her on the lips. No tongue, just warm, soft lips. Nice.

"Okay, bye."

She grinned. "Bye."

Then he headed off down the hall. She shut the door, and leaned her head against the cool wood.

"Well, I'll be damned," she whispered.

8

WHAT THE HELL am I doing? Luke waited for the elevator as he wondered if he'd lost his mind. He'd like to use the excuse that it was just a whim, a momentary lapse of judgment, but he'd had to find out her room number, leave his ski equipment with the bellman, go up to her floor, walk down the hall and knock on the door. Premeditation all the way.

He'd been thinking about her. So what? He thought about women all the time, particularly when he'd been fortunate enough to sleep with them. But it had been different this morning. How, he wasn't sure. Just different.

The elevator arrived and he rode down alone, anxious now to get out on his first run. He'd blown a good half hour in his effort to see Megan again. Damn it, he wasn't supposed to see her again. Maybe in the bar, or in the restaurant where they would smile, chat for a minute and head their separate ways. No one, in all the years he'd vacationed since he'd developed the plan, had stirred him to break his no double-dipping rule.

It didn't take him long to get his stuff and head outside. He'd bought lift tickets day one, so all he had to do was get up the hill. He checked his equipment, then caught a seat. The whole ride up he thought about Megan, about lunch and last night. By the time he reached the top of the mountain, he'd figured out that the only possible explanation was that he'd gone nuts.

He couldn't think about it anymore. This run down the mountain was one of the toughest he'd faced, and he wanted to beat his last time of 3:09:62. He wasn't competing anymore, but he still wanted to win. The discipline and the rigorous training schedule were key factors in his success, and this is where he honed the skills. Where a fall could land him in the hospital or worse. Nothing like a nice bit of life-threatening terror to get one's head out of one's ass.

He had to wait for two other guys before he could take his position at the start wand, which was cool, as he still had to wax his skis. His gaze went over to the lodge. He could see the patio from where he stood, although it was too far to make out individual faces. He didn't think she was there. Not so soon. She'd been in her robe, with her hair all bundled in that towel.

It would be an hour minimum before she came out, if she came out. Yeah, she'd come. She'd looked surprised, but pleased that he'd asked her.

Okay, so they'd have lunch. No biggie. It wasn't a commitment, and it didn't mean anything. Lots of people have lunch without it leading to the bedroom.

Discipline. He was good at that. Delayed gratification was one of the key issues that separated the men from the boys. He'd learned early that being able to wait, to have patience, made him different from almost everyone he knew. It was a little-discussed skill, but crucial. He'd forced himself to put things off, to forgo pleasures, even when there was no need. He likened it to samurai training, and in fact, had read up on the subject. He'd studied karate, and the philosophy behind it suited him.

He could have lunch with Megan. He could even relax and have a good time. Then he could say goodbye and that would be that.

It was finally his turn. He put his wax away, then got into position, lowered his goggles, tightened his grip on his poles, then started the countdown. He was going to beat his time. He knew it like he knew how to breathe. Nothing existed but him, the skis, the snow. He was ready.

MEGAN GOT A SEAT facing the Big Ben Grand Slalom run. Each of the tables on the deck had portable heaters nearby, making the air bearable, if not cozy. The waiters all wore down jackets, black stretch pants and black gloves. Very trendy, and yet, she suspected, pretty warm. Her waiter came by and she ordered cocoa. It would warm her and she wouldn't have to take off her gloves to drink it.

Her gaze went to the long, winding path that made up the Grand Slalom. She had no idea what would compel a person to ski on something so dangerous. She hated the idea of the ski lift, let alone hurtling down a mountain on two sticks. No way she'd ever get up there, not even if she'd had two good legs. Heights weren't her thing. Scuba diving. Now that was a sport she could get into. Although she'd never tried it, she'd seen enough to know that it was safe, if one followed the rules, and there was the whole buoyancy thing, which meant her leg wasn't a hand-

icap at all. Next vacation she'd go to the Bahamas
or someplace like that.

She focused on the skier whooshing down the run,
but it wasn't Luke. This guy had a red jacket, so she
felt comfortable turning away as the waiter brought
her drink. The big thermometer on the wall of the
chalet read 22 degrees. The portable heaters mitigated
that somewhat but not enough. She had on a furry
hat that covered her ears, her big coat, thick wool
socks under her pants and she'd even worn long un-
derwear. None of which helped her nose, which was
getting colder by the moment. Soon, she knew, it
would start to run. So attractive. A nice complement
to the redness that would give her that elegant Rudolf
mien. Jeez, why'd he have to pick the outdoor café?

She caught sight of a skier in black. It was him.
No doubt about it. He was circling behind the gate,
getting into position.

Her heart accelerated, and she wasn't sure if it was
worry about his daredevil ski run, or if she was all
atwitter just seeing him. Probably both.

He was there, now, goggles in place, waiting for
the big clock to start him off.

She stopped breathing when he flew out onto the
mountain. The speed of his descent made her sick. If
he fell… Oh, God, he looked amazing. Every turn
fluid and graceful, the power in his legs awesome.
He nicked the flags, became airborne on little hills,
and landed squarely on both skis. It was like watching the winter Olympics.

She caught a glimpse of the women at the table
next to hers. They were watching Luke, too. It was

impossible not to stare. This was athleticism at its purest. Beautiful and dangerous.

He rounded another curve only this time he didn't just knick the flag, he barreled into it. Her heart stopped as he fell, tumbling headfirst into the snow then sliding down the mountain in a flurry of white.

She stood, barely aware that she'd started praying. The slide went on and on, impossibly long and horrible, and oh, God, how could anyone survive such a spill? The women from the next table had gotten to their feet, too, and Megan heard one of them say, "Jesus, he's a goner."

Megan wanted to scream, but her throat had closed tight. All she could do was watch Luke flail as he hurtled down, an avalanche of flesh and bone and pain.

At last, after a lifetime of panic, he smashed into the barrier on the side of the mountain.

She wanted to run out to him, to help him, but how could she? Her stupid leg kept her a prisoner, unable to do anything at all but stand uselessly by. Thankfully, the ski patrol was right there, and for a long time, too long, they hid Luke from view, huddled around him in a cluster. Her hammering heart couldn't take much more, and she used all her willpower not to come unglued as the minutes ticked by.

Finally, the ski patrol spread out. Luke was alive. On his feet. She wasn't close enough to see if he'd been injured, but it was a good sign that they hadn't put him on a stretcher. His limbs must not be broken. At least his legs. She breathed again, a deep, burning breath.

He stood on his skis, talking to one of the ski patrol. Maybe they were waiting for a snow ambulance, or whatever they used to deploy hurt people. The front desk would undoubtedly know where the hospital was, and she could hire a car to take her.

She reached for her crutches, but stopped when she saw Luke shake the guy's hand, then ski down the mountain. Megan slid into her chair. He wasn't hurt. It was a bloody miracle. No one could have taken that spectacular a fall and skied away, but she'd seen it with her own eyes. Unbelievable.

She signaled the waiter, but kept her gaze on Luke as she ordered a shot of mescal. It wasn't a Xanex, but it would suffice.

Luke had skied off the run, and was heading down. She debated ordering him a drink, but thought she'd wait. She had no idea what he liked, other than Courvoisier.

Her hands shook as she sipped her cocoa, unfortunately cold by this time. She didn't care. She'd been scared out of her mind, and that always made her thirsty.

She nearly dropped her cup when Luke veered off to his right, turned around and caught the ski lift. He wasn't coming to join her, he was going back up the mountain! Did he have a death wish, or what?''

"Now, that's what I call macho," the woman at the next table said.

Megan shot her a glance, but she didn't seem to be making fun. In fact, she stared up at the ski lift with a faint look of hero worship.

"He nearly killed himself," her friend said.

The woman, in her thirties, Megan thought, with perfect makeup, smiled with just a touch of condescension. "But he's getting right back up on the horse, so to speak. That takes guts."

"Or an alarming lack of brain cell function," Megan interjected.

The woman laughed, as did her friend, who didn't appear to have a lick of makeup on her face. "He's a jock. What did you expect?"

"Not this. I'm sorry, it's nuts."

"I imagine he competes." The woman leaned back in her chair and crossed long, thin legs. "They don't quit unless they've broken something vital."

"I don't get it." Megan stared up at the ski lift, where Luke was nearly at the top.

"I assume you broke your leg skiing."

Megan whipped her gaze back to the next table. "Yeah. I did."

"So, you're something of a daredevil yourself."

"Trust me. I wasn't doing anything terribly dangerous. This was a fluke, a freak accident, that's all."

"Probably wouldn't have been hurt at all if you had the coordination and training some of these men have. Not that you're not coordinated, but these athletes are like machines. That's how they survive. By being in such great shape. It's pretty amazing."

"I suppose you're right. But still, it seems so unnecessary to put oneself in such danger."

"Some people," the other woman said, "have to experience very strong stimuli in order to feel anything. I'm Betsy, by the way, and this is Ellen."

"Hi. I'm Megan. And I'm supposed to be meeting that guy for lunch, so if I pass out or anything, you'll understand."

Betsy and Ellen exchanged a look.

"So he's yours?" Ellen asked.

"No. He's not. But he is supposed to be my lunch date. If he lives."

"He's a major babe," Ellen said. "I've seen him at the lodge. You're a lucky gal."

Megan flexed her toes, which was pretty much all she could do with that leg. "That's me. Lucky all over."

"He's at the gate," Betsy said.

Megan whipped around to see Luke bending over his skis, staring down that long, horrible run. Her adrenaline spiked instantly, and she gripped the arms of her chair so hard she thought she might break them. Why did he have to do this? What in hell was he trying to prove?

Maybe Betsy was right. Maybe Luke couldn't feel anything unless his life was at risk. She'd read something about that in *Cosmo* or *Jane* or a magazine like that. Adrenaline junkies, that's what they'd called them. If that were the case, then she should be grateful he was only a Man To Do. She avoided potentially lethal experiences as a rule. Having had one up close and personal was enough for her, thank you.

Luke took off like a bullet out of a rifle, the speed dazzling and terrifying. Watching skiing on television didn't capture it at all. With every heartbeat, he was at another flag, turning, leaning, narrowly missing disaster. She wanted to close her eyes, but the best she could manage was to put her hand in front of her face and peek through her fingers.

She thought about his body, how beautiful it was, like a living sculpture. Perfect. The risk seemed too great. She had firsthand knowledge of how he could end up, and she couldn't see Luke adjusting to a brace or, God forbid, a wheelchair. He wouldn't be able to tolerate the pity, let alone the very real logistical problems he'd have to face every day.

Buildings without ramps, door so heavy it was impossible to open them from the chair. Not to mention the idiots who thought being in a wheelchair meant deafness or being mentally disabled. She thought of the times people had spoken to her in huge, loud voices. Once, some ass of a woman had patted her on her head! It had been really, really hard not to bite that hand.

Luke neared the bottom of the run, the last two gates. She widened her fingers and held her breath until he'd done it. Leveled off and put on his brakes with a shower of powder. Her hand dropped and she leaned back in her chair, willing her body to calm down. Her drink was on the table, and she tossed it back like a sailor on leave. The liquor burned all the way down, but it was a good burn.

She tried to remember the last time she'd had a drink when it was still daylight. College. After finals. Oh, and playing the Bob Newhart game. Jeez, that took her back. A whole group of her friends used to sit in the lounge and watch reruns of the old comedy. Every time someone said Bob, they had to take a drink. First one to quit or pass out lost. She lost quite often.

June, however, won an alarming number of times. She was one of those people who could drink like a fish and stay sober. Okay, not sober so much as upright. But it was very impressive.

"He made it."

Megan turned to her neighbors. "I still think it's not worth it. But then, there are lots of sports I don't get. Boxing. I mean, please. If I wanted to see people beating the crap out of each other, I'd go to the Bronx."

Betsy laughed. Ellen smiled, but shook her head. "Ask him. Find out what he gets from doing it. Maybe he'll surprise you."

"Good idea. I will."

Betsy stood, and Megan saw they'd finished their meal awhile ago. "Let us know what he says. We're here until next Sunday."

"Okay. It was nice to meet you."

"You, too." Ellen grabbed her purse from the chair next to her. "Take care of that leg."

Megan nodded, smiling. Thinking that she'd be delighted to take care of her leg. Only, there was no care to take. Once the cast came off, it would be the same old same old. But for today, she had a lunch date with a major babe.

Her gaze went back to the mountain. She searched for Luke, looking for his black coat. She'd been checking out the various wardrobes of the skiers since she'd arrived, some ideas germinating in the back of her mind. Ever since she'd done that ski shoot back in Manhattan, she'd been intrigued with the design aspects of the gear. In fact, seeing Luke ready for action this morning had given her a specific target. She got out her pad and a charcoal and started sketching, using Luke's body as her model, focusing on warmth, water repellent fabric and ease of movement. The cold disappeared as she lost herself to the drawing.

LUKE SKIED OVER to the rest area at the bottom of the hill and found a bench. It would take a while for his heart rate to decelerate and his breathing to become normal. He used the time to go over the run in his head, think about what he could do better next time. Then, as he was taking off his skis, he thought about his fall. Jeez, he'd been lucky to get out of that one with nothing broken. The last time he'd slammed like that, it had been the fault of his equipment. This time, he had nothing to blame but himself.

He'd been distracted. The one thing an athlete absolutely can't afford. He'd been halfway down the run and he'd wondered if Megan was at the café, and that was all it took. He'd screwed up his turn, lost his balance. Yet another living illustration of why focus was the most important thing in his life. No distractions. Distractions caused disasters.

He looked over at the lodge, but from this angle he couldn't see the outdoor patio. She'd probably be there by now. Hopefully, she hadn't gotten there till his last run. He wanted to impress her. Which was weird, because he wasn't going to see her again after they finished lunch.

Which brought him back to his original question. What was he doing having lunch with her?

He took off his goggles and rubbed his eyes. He liked her. Great. No problem there. He wasn't in love or anything close to it, he just clicked with her, that's all. He'd asked her to lunch because he wanted her company. No big deal there, either. Just because he'd never asked a woman out twice didn't mean he was losing it. In fact, maybe it was a good thing.

He was on vacation. So was she. Things happened

on vacation that were outside the normal scope of his life. As long as he kept this change of plan in perspective, there should be no problem.

The bottom line was, he did want to see her again, and he wasn't at all sure lunch would be enough. He didn't have to know why.

The question then became was it going to distract him more to see her, or try to stop thinking about her?

He shook his head, not at all comfortable with the whole scenario. He should let it go. Have lunch with her, and say goodbye. But something told him it wouldn't be that easy.

Dammit, the sex had been good, but not that good. She'd had that damn cast, which made things trickier. He'd had to take it into consideration, being mindful of what she could and couldn't do.

He grunted and sat up. Interesting. He thought of a bunch of positions she wouldn't be able to do. And several she would. A few he'd have to try to see if they could.

A challenge. Now it was starting to make more sense. It was because she was in the cast, that's all. Something new. Different.

He relaxed. Now that he understood why she intrigued him, it was a pretty straight shot to his next move. He had five more nights at the lodge. He could afford to spend a couple of those with Megan, as long as he remembered what was important. Wanting to be with her again was like wanting a hot-fudge sundae when he was in training. The longer he tried to ignore it, the more intense the craving became. The only way to get over it was to indulge. Eat the damn thing and then move on.

He got up and headed for the lodge, feeling much better now that he was armed with a plan.

9

MEGAN LOOKED UP from her pad as Luke walked into the café. He'd left his equipment somewhere, and his dark hair was slicked back, making him look dangerous and sexy. His cheekbones were truly sensational. She'd never thought that about any other man, but damn, combined with his lips and those eyes, he was right up there with Brad Pitt and Benjamin Bratt. He had a magnetism about him that she'd seen in a few celebrities but hardly any civilians. Of course he did well at being a broker. The man inspired confidence. And made her nipples hard. A heady combination indeed.

"Hey," he said, his grin more charming than she'd remembered. And she had a damn good memory.

"Hi."

He kissed her lightly on the cheek, then sat down in the chair next to her. "Hope you haven't been waiting too long."

"Nope," she said, making sure her voice was steady, as if his little peck on the cheek hadn't thrilled her down to her toes. "Just long enough to watch you tear up the mountain. That was one hell of a spill."

"You saw that, huh?"

"Yeah. I saw it."

"It wasn't all that bad. I've had worse."

"And yet you continue to ski."

He looked at her as if she'd said something odd. "Well, sure."

"Why?"

"What do you mean?"

"Why do you take risks like that?"

He picked up his menu, gave it a cursory glance then put it down. "It's the challenge, I suppose. If it was easy, everybody would do it."

"Hmm." She thought about that while he signaled the waiter.

Luke ordered a he-man lunch of steak and fries, and she got the bowl of clam chowder. Once they were alone again, he scooted his chair closer.

"But I suppose, after your accident..."

She panicked for a moment, wondering how he'd found out about the car crash, and then she remembered her cast and gave herself a mental *thwap* on the head. "Well, it's no fun to be broken."

"Not broken," he said. "Temporarily wounded. Big difference."

She forced a smile. "Huge."

"How did it happen?"

"What?"

He nodded toward the cast.

"Oh." The panic welled again, but not as badly as a moment ago. She'd thought about this question, asked one of her friends who actually did ski what a plausible scenario would be. "I met a tree."

"Ouch."

"You got that right."

"How did they get you out?"

"The tree was pretty conveniently located. A tree any observant person would have missed by a mile."

"Ah. Well, that's good, though. I mean, that you didn't have to be coptered out or anything."

"Sounds as if you have."

"Yeah. Once. Broke my collarbone. My right arm. I was in Vermont, and I'd been hotdogging. It was just before the trials."

"What trials?"

"The Olympics. I was going for the team."

"Oh, no."

He sighed, and she could see that the disappointment was still very raw. His eyes, so alive and vibrant, dulled as if from an internal cloud. "That was my one shot. I never got that close again."

"I'm sorry."

He shrugged and pulled a smile from somewhere. "No sweat. I've won my share of competitions."

"Cool. You have trophies and everything?"

"Yep."

"I think that's excellent. I'm all in favor of trophies. I think you should get them for everything. For making a deadline, for getting Jimmy Choo shoes at half price."

He laughed, and with that, the light came back to his eyes. Pleased, she laughed, too, enjoying the moment, feeling great. Feeling like she was in the best possible seat with the best possible person. All was glorious in her universe except for her nose, which had reached running temperature. She dabbed at it with her napkin, hoping he'd think she was aiming for her mouth. Nothing turns a guy on faster than a runny nose, but she didn't like to make things too easy.

"Speaking of Olympics," he said, "I was thinking."

"About?"

The waiter arrived then, so the conversation was put on hold. Once they had their meals, and Luke had eaten several bites of his rare steak, he picked the ball up again. "I was thinking," he repeated, "about your leg."

"My leg?" Panic again. This was not good. Her poor little adrenal glands weren't used to this pace.

"Yeah. I mean, given the situation, there are certain restrictions."

"I wish I could say I knew what you're talking about, but—"

"Wait. I have a point. I swear."

"Okay."

"For example," he said, looking at her with a sly grin, "it wouldn't be easy for you to be on top."

"Ah." The lightbulb went off, and with it, her panic eased as her embarrassment took center stage. "Those kind of restrictions."

"Right. But that doesn't mean someone creative couldn't work around the, uh, issue."

"It doesn't?"

He shook his head. Ate some more steak. "However, I don't think the subject has been researched very well. I've certainly never read anything about it."

"Really? I just read 'Postcast Coitus' in *Reader's Digest*. The large-print version."

"Cute," he said. "Very cute. But I'm being serious here."

"Oh." She frowned and looked at him through narrowed eyes. "Sorry."

"It's okay."

"So this would be a humanitarian effort then?"

"Absolutely. A lot of people break their legs, right? Don't they deserve to get their rocks off? Aren't they entitled to equal nooky?"

"Wait," she said, "I think I'm going to cry. I've never heard anything so selfless in my life."

"Stop, you're making me blush."

She rolled her eyes. "Right."

"Hey, I think it's a worthy endeavor. You have a few days. I have a few days. We could see just how creative we could be."

She tried to get her head around his proposal. She'd been convinced it had been a one-night stand. Utterly sure. So what had changed?

"Unless you have other plans," he said, sitting back in his chair as if he was ready to bolt. "That's not a problem. It's your vacation and you—"

"No, it's not that. I don't have any other plans. Frankly, I'm a little surprised."

He relaxed his shoulders a little, but his expression was puzzled. "You know what? I'm surprised, too. I don't do this. Not on vacation."

"You don't sleep with women? I find that hard to believe."

"No, that's not what I meant. I don't sleep with women twice."

Her brow rose. "Really?"

He nodded. "It's not personal or anything. It's just safer. With the master plan and all."

"Retiring at forty?"

"Right. The whole deal is contingent on staying loose until things are in place."

"After retirement?"

"Yeah. So I don't put myself in a position where things can get out of hand."

"I see."

"I hadn't planned on asking you to lunch."

"What changed?"

He looked at her earnestly. "I keep thinking about you."

"Oh."

"So rather than fight it, I thought I'd take the opportunity to make a difference in the world."

She grinned, but it was more from feeling overwhelmingly flattered than his attempt to lighten the mood. "You're a regular Albert Schweitzer."

"Hey, it's a rough job, but someone's got to do it."

"Hmm."

He touched her hand. The first touch since he'd sat down. What it did to her insides was way outside the safety zone. "Come on, Megan. What do you say? I dare you."

"Oh, we're back to that, are we?"

"Why not? Hell, we're on vacation, right?"

"You bet."

"So let's give it a go. Just for tonight. What do you say?"

Inside, she was shouting, "Yes, yes! Hot diggity dog, yes!" But outside, she kept her smile subdued, her expression thoughtful. "I don't know," she said, drawing out the words. "I did have a really excellent time last night...."

"So, what's the problem?"

She studied him hard, as if basing her decision on his character rather than his incredibly hot body. "All right. Let's see what you can come up with."

His grin started strong but faded quickly.

"What's wrong?"

He shook his head. "Nothing. How about you come by my room tonight around seven. We'll have dinner."

"Dinner?"

"Room service."

"Cool."

"And then dessert." His eyebrows arched suggestively, letting her know she was on the menu.

She blushed, the heat warming her all over. "Are you going back out there?"

He nodded, looking over at the grand slalom run. "Oh, yeah. It's early. The sun starts to go down around five-thirty. And I got a late start this morning."

"Fair enough. But do me a favor. Don't get killed. It would be hell to get reservations for dinner so late."

"Deal." He squeezed her hand, then went back to his meal, eating with gusto.

She watched him for a while, enjoying his appetite. In her world, lettuce leaves and poached chicken breasts were a Sunday feast, which was depressing after a while. The models used cigarettes and coffee as their main food groups, and the designers and photographers weren't much better. Emaciation was de rigueur, and she'd often pondered her own relatively normal eating habits, wondering if her craving for Twinkies doomed her forever.

She'd tried to diet, to be like the women at work, but she'd given it up when she realized her leg cancelled out any skinny bonus points. As June said, "Screw it with authority."

"You don't like the soup?"

She blinked herself back to the table, to Luke. "No, it's fine." To illustrate, she took a big spoonful, only to find the chowder was now cold, and that clam gazpacho would never make it onto her favorite foods list. The waiter wasn't around to heat up her bowl, but that was okay. She wasn't all that hungry. "Tell me more about your master plan," she said, relaxing back in her seat. "It sounds to me like it's been in the works a long time."

He swallowed the last bite of steak as he confirmed her guess with a nod. "Ever since my father died."

"Oh?"

"He worked his ass off his whole life, six, sometimes seven days a week. He'd come home beat, and then he'd have to fix dinner and do laundry, that kind of thing. Whenever he did have time off, he used it to sleep."

"Ouch. Tough."

"Yeah. Dad had been an athlete when he was young. A baseball player. He'd been good, too. Got in the minors, and everyone who saw him pitch said he was good enough for the show. But then my mother got pregnant, and he got the job at the hardware store."

"He must have been very proud of your success."

"He wasn't around for most of it. The bitch was, he'd had all these plans for when he retired. He'd talk about it every chance he got. He wanted to move somewhere near water. The Ozarks. Get himself a little place so he could fish to his heart's content. He had the whole thing worked out. Every detail. Only he died. He hadn't fished in fifteen years when he had the heart attack."

"And you don't want that to happen to you."

"Damn straight. I'm not going to let anything stop me from living out my dreams. I'm good with money, and if I'm careful, I'll be set. No worries."

"Life has a way of messing with the best laid plans. I mean, what if something comes up?"

"Like what?"

"I don't know. A major downturn in the economy?"

"I'm diversified. Shouldn't be a problem."

"Okay. But what about your personal life? Marriage, kids. That's going to take some modification, no?"

"There'll be plenty of time to get married after I retire. And I've decided not to have kids."

"Really?"

He nodded. "I've thought a lot about it, and I think it's the right decision for me. I don't have any burning desire to pass on my genes or anything. And frankly, I'm probably too selfish to be a good father."

"Good for you. I think more people should think about it carefully before they go forth and multiply."

"What about you?"

"And kids?"

He nodded.

"I'm not sure yet. It's going to take a lot of energy and commitment to start my own design business. I can't imagine it would be easier with a baby."

"No biological clock ticking?"

"Not so I'd notice. But maybe that'll change when I hit my thirties. Who knows? I'm trying to keep my options open."

"Makes sense."

"I like to think so."

He drank down his water, finished the last of his fries, then leaned back and took a long, deep breath.

"Satisfied?" she asked.

"Yeah. It's good."

"The food?"

He shook his head. "Life. All of it. I'm damn lucky, and I know it."

"I envy your confidence."

"You're not too shabby, yourself. I can see you making it."

"I don't know. It's rough out there."

"Sure it is. But that's what makes it worthwhile."

"Sometimes people fail through no fault of their own."

"I don't buy that."

"No?"

"It's just like skiing. If you fall down, you have to get right back up. Learn from your mistakes, and go for it."

"That's pretty hard to do if the mistake is a broken leg."

"Yeah, but that's temporary. As soon as the cast is off, you can try it again."

She looked toward the mountain, at all the healthy people swooshing about in the snow. She'd wanted to learn to ski, but now, it was too late. She smiled as she turned back to Luke. "Is the grand slalom your specialty?"

He nodded, clearly not bothered by her change of subject. "Yeah. I do regular slalom sometimes. But mostly, I do the grand." He picked up the bill and reached for his jacket.

"Let me get this," she said.

He gave her a sharp look. "Not a chance. I asked you. And don't forget. Seven tonight, okay?"

"I'll be there."

10

HE HAD TWO MORE RUNS before the sun gave it up. Two incredible runs, the last breaking his best time by seconds. He'd been right to invite Megan to dinner. His focus on the mountain had been laser sharp, and he'd kicked ass.

Exhilarated and pleasantly achy, he headed for his room, aware only peripherally of the other skiers with the same agenda. Until he got to the elevator.

A woman in white, skintight leggings and a form-fitting sweater smiled at him as he pressed the up button. "You're extraordinarily good," she said, her voice higher than he expected. Breathy.

"Thank you."

"I watched your last run. It was gorgeous."

His radar locked in like a heat-seeking missile to the invitation in her eyes. Any other trip, he'd have been giving himself a mental high five. She was a knockout. Her long blond hair pushed back by a white headband showed off her perfect skin and pale blue eyes. She was just his type. Legs up to there, tight butt, perfect breasts. He smiled at her, but it wasn't the come-on it should have been. Megan was who he wanted to be with. Go figure. "I don't know how gorgeous it was," he said, "but it felt damn good."

"I can only imagine. I've never dared try the grand slalom. I'm just a season off the bunny slope."

"I'll bet you're hell on skis."

She took a tiny step forward and touched his arm. "I'm not, but you're sweet to say so."

He wasn't sure what to do. Normally, he'd have moved in to close the deal. The touch was the clincher, so he'd have no hesitation. He could have stepped back and looked away, which would have ended things pronto, but this thing with Megan was probably good for tonight only. He might want to pick this up again tomorrow. "Well, tell you what," he said, just as the elevator door opened. "I'll keep an eye out for you tomorrow, and we'll just see."

She smiled invitingly, and she went into the cab. Two other skiers and a bellman went in before him, separating him from the blonde.

"That would be great," she said, undaunted by the elevator silence rule. "I'm Peggy."

"Nice to meet you," he said, looking at her over the shoulder of the bellman. "I'm Luke."

The silence fell again as the doors opened on the fourth floor. A couple, young and laughing, squished everyone to the back. On the next stop, Peggy got out, but not before she touched his hand, slipping him a piece of paper. "Nice to meet you, too," she said, and then the doors closed.

The bellman looked at the paper in his hand, then met his gaze. His smile was conspiratorial and somewhat lecherous. Luke, who appreciated the game as much as any man, wasn't one to beat his chest. He looked up at the numbers, impatient now to reach his floor.

When he got to his room, he put his equipment away, then got right into the shower. It felt amazing. The hot water eased his shoulder muscles and warmed up all the cold that had seeped into his bones. He rubbed his shoulder, sore since his spill, but nothing tragic. In fact, the ache felt kind of good. Like a badge of his willingness to take it to the limit.

He closed his eyes, letting his tension run down the drain. His thoughts drifted from his last run to the rumble in his stomach, to the evening ahead. He pictured Megan in his bed, naked and waiting. He'd promised her fireworks. So what was he going to do? Damn, there were a lot of possibilities.

His cock thickened as he went over the short list. Lay her on her side and enter her from the back. No, they'd kind of done that. He needed something more spectacular. Ah, lifting her onto the wet bar, resting her bad leg on the back of a chair, spreading her open like a juicy oyster. His hand moved down his stomach as he thought of all the things he could do. It wouldn't take much to make him come, but he forced himself to stop. Used to be, in his early twenties, that he'd want an orgasm before a date so he'd last longer. Now that he'd hit his thirties, he didn't bounce back quite so quickly.

He got busy with the shampoo, directed his thoughts to dinner. He wanted everything ready by the time she got here. He'd order several things to be sure she'd find something appealing. Wine, of course, and he'd light a fire. He'd also put a blanket on the wet bar. Damn, he was a good Samaritan.

MEGAN TURNED OFF the water in the shower, and grabbed a towel from the rack. She wrapped her hair,

turban-style, then plucked another of the thick, white
towels to dry herself with. A few moments later, she
stood in front of her foggy mirror, debating her wardrobe.

She'd brought one skirt with her, and tonight might
just be the perfect time to wear it. It was a lot easier
to get naked wearing the skirt than pants. But would
it make her seem easy?

She laughed. Right. As if she'd been playing it
hard to get. The skirt it was.

On top, she'd wear her silk blouse and her demi-
bra. She shifted to her left, grabbing onto the sink for
support. Damn cast. Of course, without the damn cast
she wouldn't be primping for a hot date, but still, it
was awkward and more uncomfortable than she'd
imagined.

She felt even more graceless than usual. The brace
was no picnic, but she was used to it. She knew what
she could and couldn't do.

The mirror was still too foggy to see in. She
reached for her blow dryer to clear it up but she
changed her mind. Instead, she used both hands to
balance against the sink, then lifted her bad leg up
until she hooked her heel on the edge. It was a tough
stretch, and she felt the muscles in her thigh protest.
Taking a deep breath, she relaxed, and bent over her
leg, like she'd done years ago in ballet class. The
barre had been shorter, of course. And she hadn't
been crippled back then.

Sense memories filled her with her past. Her most
vivid dreams were about running, about dancing. In
her sleep, she was whole and strong and nothing

could stop her. It was always hard to wake up from those dreams.

Her thigh protested more urgently, and she straightened, ready to bring her leg down. Only, it wasn't quite so simple. She tugged, pulled. Nothing. Her heel was stuck on the lip of the counter. Great. She'd be stuck like this forever, and Luke would come looking for her, and he wouldn't hear her yelling from behind the bathroom door. Worse, he would, and he'd find her like this.

She focused all her energy on her leg, and after a mighty effort, it came down. She sighed, grateful for small miracles.

Best to keep her gymnastics to a minimum while she put on her makeup and dressed. She had an hour and a half till dinner, and she wanted to relax.

HE WORE JEANS, a long sleeved V-neck gray sweater and socks. She thought he quite possibly was the best-looking man in the northern hemisphere.

"Wow, you look great," he said, taking her overnight bag, then stepping back to let her in.

"Thank you." She'd learned that trick from Christy Brinkly. Before, when handed a compliment, she'd stammer and blush and discount whatever had been said. Christy had taught her to simply smile and say thank you. She'd said the important thing was to make sure whoever was giving the compliment felt heard. That the words mattered. It had been great advice and although she still felt as if she should say something modest, she held back.

Her thoughts shifted gears the second she was inside his suite, staring at the table set up in the middle of the room. Luke had ordered dinner, she saw, although the food was covered by silver domes, so she couldn't see what it was. She could see the pink roses, amazing in midwinter, and the candles, amazing any time. Long pink tapers in silver holders sat glowing on the white-clothed table, and several votives shimmered around the dimly lit room. Sinatra sang quietly in the background about being bewitched, bothered and bewildered. Megan understood completely.

Although she'd had her share, small share, of dates, she'd never had anything like this. Her past encounters had been of the cheap wine and sturdy couch variety. Luke had a bottle of vintage Armagnac, and the setting was elegant seduction.

"Here," he said, putting the wine down on the counter. "Take a seat. I'll get your crutches."

She obeyed, grateful to sit in the comfy dining chair. It was upholstered in a rich burgundy brocade, and it hadn't been in the room last night, so he must have ordered it along with the meal. Once she'd gotten comfortable, he grabbed her crutches and put them against the wall by the wet bar. He took her bag into the bedroom, then came back to the wine. "I wasn't sure what you liked," he said. "So there are a few things to choose from. Go ahead and look."

She took the cover off the closest plate. Lobster tails. Big ones. Lemon wedges and small cups of melted butter completed the entrée. "Wow," she said. "I love it."

"Great," he said, then there was a pop as the cork came loose. He filled her glass, then his. After he put the bottle into the chilled ice bucket next to the table, he turned to her. "I think I forgot something."

"What?"

"This," he said, as he leaned down to capture her lips in a scorching kiss. She leaned back as she reacquainted herself with the feel and taste of him. Peppermint and heat, soft lips and darting tongue. She moaned with pleasure, and he chuckled, the sound deep and rich and filled with promise. He pulled back, and she almost grabbed him by the sweater and forced him to continue, but stopped herself. The evening was young, and he'd gone to a great deal of trouble.

"Go on." He nodded at the next covered dish.

A perfect herbed rack of lamb, complete with little white skirts on the bones for easy handling, nestled in a bed of wild rice. It smelled like heaven.

"One more," he said, taking his seat next to her.

She uncovered the last dish and found a large helping of pasta with some kind of fabulous smelling meat sauce. A chunk of fresh parmesan with a mini grater rested against the platter. "Luke, this is sensational. How can I possibly choose?"

"Don't. Have it all. This is a night for indulgence."

"If I ate all of this, even sharing it with you, the rest of the night wouldn't be in the least romantic."

He laughed. "Then just take a little of each. But leave room for dessert."

She shook her head. "Decadent. Hedonistic. Self-indulgent. I love it."

He waggled his brows at her as he gave her an

impish grin. "Let's eat before this decadent spread gets cold."

She spread her napkin on her lap, dizzy with the opulence out in front of her. She was pretty dazzled by the meal, too. But if he'd ordered hot dogs and fries, she'd have been just as happy.

He started in on the pasta, and she began with the lobster. It was so delicious, she made the yummy noise, causing him to chuckle again. She loved the sound. The way his eyes crinkled and his lips curved up ever so slightly made her smile. She couldn't help but stare at him when she wasn't actively cutting or stabbing a morsel of food. He had a fluid way about his movements. An economy of motion she attributed to his athletic prowess. It had been the same in bed. His hands seemed to glide over her body finding the exact spot that most wanted to be touched. A frisson shimmied down her back, nesting between her thighs, and she wriggled a bit on the chair.

"Are you cold?"

"No, not at all. The fire really keeps the room warm."

"Too much?"

She shook her head. "It's all perfect."

"Good. I want you to be comfortable."

She smiled, dunked a piece of lobster in butter sauce. "So how was the rest of your day?"

"Great. I cut my time by a few seconds."

"Congratulations."

He grinned happily. "Thanks."

"No more spills?"

"Nope. And I wasn't even all that banged up. A bruise here and there, that's all."

"Clearly, I'm a lot whinier than you. I tend to milk my injuries to the hilt."

"You do not. You've hardly mentioned your leg."

"Oh, well, that's different. Haven't you noticed it's the paper cuts that hurt the worst?"

"True. Wonder why that is?"

"I've wondered myself."

His grin turned mischievous. "Maybe after I complete this study, I'll turn my attention to the paper cut conundrum."

"Ah, so this isn't a one-time thing, eh? You've decided to go into philanthropy full-time?"

"Not full-time, but I do think I have a duty, don't you?"

"Absolutely."

"A lot's riding on the outcome of this study. I mean, if I expect to be in the running for a Nobel and all."

"You're not going to need visual aids, are you?"

"Hmm." He traded plates for the lamb chops, and put the pasta near her. "I hadn't thought about it, but I think you've got something there." He looked toward the bedroom. "I have a camera here somewhere."

"You take a picture, you die."

"Spoilsport."

"That's me."

"Okay, so maybe we'll go with illustrations. You can do them. Tastefully, of course."

She put her fork down and frowned. "Wait a minute. Tastefully? I was under the impression none of what we're about to do would be tasteful. Jeez. I was all ready for a night of debauchery, and you're giving me tasteful?''

Luke nearly spit his wine all over the table. Megan cracked up, happy to have lightened the mood. Not that she was tense, exactly. She was more like… like… Oh, hell. She was tense. Tense, scared, excited, giddy and a whole bunch of other words she couldn't think of at the moment because Luke had stopped coughing and his hand was on her thigh. Her giggles faded as he gave her a gentle yet meaningful squeeze.

''You want debauchery? I can do that.''

''Uh, Luke. That was a joke. Ha-ha. Funny, you know?''

''Really?'' he said, arching his brow in disbelief. ''I wonder.''

''You don't have to. Wonder, I mean. I was kidding.''

His hand moved up an inch, settling on the middle of her thigh. ''A thousand apologies, but I fear I can't take your word for that. It adds a whole new layer to the investigation, and I'd be remiss to let it slide.''

The way he looked at her was debauchery personified. His nostrils flared, his pupils dilated until only a trace of midnight-blue remained on the edges. His lips, those incredible lips, curved up in a wicked smile that made her long for the tension of a few moments ago.

''But first,'' he said, his voice lower, gravely, ''we need to finish dinner.''

She wanted to finish eating almost as much as she wanted to frolic naked in the snow. But she forced herself to take a bite, then another. It helped that the food was ambrosial, but still. She would have been happy with a glass or two of the wine.

He ate with the same enthusiasm she'd seen at lunch, only he did it one-handed. The other, friskier hand had set up camp on her leg. Squeezing, rubbing, inching higher and higher, and didn't he just look like innocence itself.

When she took another sip of wine, he grew bolder still. His fingers slid down, pulling the material of her skirt with him, until he was nestled between her legs.

"Cold, are we?" she asked.

"Hmm?"

"I assume you're trying to warm your hand. Or perhaps you've misplaced something?"

He grinned. "How'd you know? I've lost this, uh, thing, and I swear it's here somewhere."

"And what would this *thing* be?"

He fought to regain that little boy innocence, but he wasn't very successful. "I'd tell you if I could. Honest. But I'm afraid that's not possible."

"Because...?"

"Are you gonna hog all the lobster?"

"Nice try, Ace."

Ignoring her prod, he moved the lamb to the middle of the table, then lifted the lobster neatly. It was quite something considering his other hand was inching toward the promised land.

"Luke."

"Hush," he said. "Try a chop."

"I'm just supposed to ignore what you're doing?"

"Hell, no. You're supposed to enjoy it."

"Oh," she said, nodding. "I see."

"Good. I'm glad we cleared that up."

"You're a piece of work, Mr. Webster."

"Why, thank you."

"How do you know it was a compliment?"

He gave her a dazzling smile worthy of Tom Cruise himself. "What else could it be?"

"You really need to work on that whole self-confidence thing. I hear they have classes at NYU."

"Nah. I don't like teaching."

She shook her head, and treated him to one of her patented eye rolls. "Men amaze me. They really do."

He ate a piece of lobster, and chewed with his eyes closed. When he looked at her again, he seemed genuinely puzzled. "What do you mean?"

"Men are just odd. I've really never met a guy who didn't think he was God's gift. I mean, a guy can have a beer gut the size of a bowling ball, and he'll traipse around naked as the day he was born, certain every woman in the western world wants his bod."

"That's not self-confidence," Luke said. "That's psychotic delusion. Which is, I'll admit, one of the more useful traits we males share."

"So you admit it?"

"Oh, yeah. It's pleasant in our world, Megan. The dishes disappear after we eat. The clothes miraculously clean themselves after two weeks in the hamper. You should try it sometime. You'd be amazed."

"I'll bet."

He finished off his glass of wine, then poured himself another, topping off her glass at the same time. "But let's not talk of dirty dishes tonight. We have better things to do."

"Right. Like finding whatever the hell you're looking for between my legs."

He waggled his brows. "I think I'm about to hit pay dirt."

And then his fingers went that last inch.

11

SHE JUMPED, somehow not expecting him to really do it. Certainly not expecting the way he made himself at home.

He didn't grope, which was something of a trick given his position and hers. No, it was more like a tickle, a tease, rubbing her skirt against her panties with just enough friction to make her gasp.

"Warm," he said, his eyelids lowering to half-mast.

She swallowed, remembered to breathe. "I, uh, thought you said there was dessert."

"There is."

She closed her eyes. It was an effort not to grab his wrist, stop the intimate rubbing. Not because she wasn't enjoying it, but there was a large element of oddness to the situation, which made her self-conscious. She wasn't sure what she was supposed to do. Lean back, and let him go to town? Continue to eat as if he wasn't touching her *right there?* Reach over and return the favor?

Luke solved the problem for her. Never pausing with his left hand, he twirled some pasta with his right, then lifted the fork. She pulled the bite off with her lips, and chewed. Even though she was incredibly preoccupied, she still swooned at the perfect sauce.

She moaned with pleasure, from the food as well as his touch. But she still had to force herself not to stop him.

"You like?"

She nodded. "But…"

"What?"

"Nothing."

"Come on, Megan. It's obviously something." He stopped moving his fingers. "Am I making you uncomfortable?"

She hesitated. She wanted him to stop, and she didn't.

"Truth," he whispered.

She gazed into his eyes, and his openness swung the vote. "All right," she said. "Truth. I'm not sure what to do here. And I don't seem to be able to relax the way I'd like to."

He didn't say anything. He simply moved his hand back to the top of her thigh. Then he leaned slowly toward her until his lips brushed against her own. Lingering there, his warm breath slipping inside her, he said, "We'll pick this up later." He kissed her again, harder, and then he leaned back.

"Thank you," she said.

"No problem. We've got the rest of the night to find things we both want to do."

"It's not that I didn't like it—"

He held up a hand. "It's okay. I mean it. I'm glad you said something. I want the truth. My ego, while larger than it should be, is surprisingly capable of handling the fact that not everything I do is magic."

"You're not off by much."

"Good."

"For the record, I'd just like to say that I'm having an excellent time."

"Even better."

She patted his leg, then had another sip of wine.

"Do you want some more pasta?"

"I do, but then I won't have room for dessert."

"Ah, okay. Good point." He stood, went to the wet bar and picked up a plate that she hadn't seen in the sink. "Dessert."

"What is it?"

He came back to the table, moved his plate and hers to the other side of the table, then uncovered the new dish with a flourish.

Two slices of a gorgeously dark, rich chocolate cake sat between beautifully sculpted butter cream roses.

"Oh, my."

"I hope you like chocolate. I didn't get anything else."

"No, I love it."

He smiled, reached below the table and pulled out two dessert plates from the cart. He served her a slice, complete with rose, and then himself.

She took a bite, and the cake melted in her mouth, filling her with sugary bliss. It was by far the best cake she'd ever had. "This is unbelievable."

"It's called Death By Chocolate, and it's a specialty here."

"You should do this for a living," she said.

"What?"

"Order dinners. You'd make a fortune. All those poor fools choosing dishes willy-nilly. Talk about a humanitarian effort."

He grinned. "Yeah, but on the other hand, I also like liver and onions. So there would always be that element of risk."

"What's life without risk?"

"My point, exactly."

She concentrated on her cake, savoring every delicious bite. It was so odd to find herself here, eating this amazing meal with this amazing man. She still couldn't get over the fact that she'd told him she was uncomfortable. She never did that. Not with guys, at least. She'd never been comfortable enough to be this honest.

Absurdly, she'd always thought if she told a guy she wasn't happy with some move, that he'd get upset and leave. Of course that was nonsense. Why hadn't she seen it before?

Another bite of cake, and she no longer cared. The hell with every other date, every other man. Luke was hers tonight. All hers.

"What are you laughing at?" he asked.

"Nothing, really. Just enjoying myself."

"I'm glad you liked the dinner."

"The dinner has been great. But that's not what I was referring to."

He smiled, took a final bite of cake, then leaned back in his chair and sighed. "What do you say we take our wine into the bedroom and get naked."

She laughed. "We've just finished eating."

"Hey, it's not like I'm asking you to go swimming."

"Tell you what. Why don't you let me freshen up, then we'll go from there."

"Fair enough." He stood and went for her crutches.

Once she was on her feet, heading for the bathroom, the butterflies in her tummy started fluttering like crazy. It didn't seem to matter that it wasn't her first time with him. Go figure.

Luke pushed the food cart against the wall in the hallway, then went back inside the suite. Megan was still in the bathroom. He made himself useful by pouring brandy into two snifters and putting them next to the couch. He'd thought better of heading straight to the bedroom. He didn't want to overwhelm Megan. He wanted her comfortable, relaxed and primed for action. In his experience, most women liked a slow seduction, even when they'd been real clear about the outcome.

He could do that. In fact, he liked foreplay almost as much as the act if he was with someone stimulating.

He'd worried that once they were eating, he'd realize he'd made a mistake seeing her again. He sure as hell needn't have worried.

Watching her eat had nearly made him come, which hadn't happened to him since high school. He hadn't actually orgasmed in his school cafeteria watching Janice Mitchner suck on her Popsicle, but that's only because he'd gotten the hell out of there and found himself a nice private bathroom stall. He didn't miss those days of unpredictable hard-ons. They would spring up unannounced at the worst possible times.

There was that time he was at the board in chemistry, and Ms. Elgin, his teacher, had brushed his hand. It wasn't a sexy touch, or a come-on or anything. In fact, it was an accident that she probably didn't even notice. He, on the other hand, got the woody from hell. He tried to hide, by working on his equation, but how many times could he erase the same stupid numbers? He'd been sent back to his seat, and never been more grateful for a dressing-down.

The adolescent hormone-fest had gotten more manageable in his late twenties, and he'd thought those issues were over forever when he hit thirty.

Evidently not.

He changed the CD in the boom box to Nat "King" Cole. His voice was as smooth as the brandy. Everything was almost perfect.

Luke cut off the lights, lit a couple of candles, then he got the thick, white towel he'd stashed, folded it in half, and spread it on the counter of the wet bar. He could see her there, perched naked, gripping the edge of the counter as he rocked her world. Damn.

The bathroom door opened, and she spotted him, her brows lifting in surprise.

"I figured we'd have a brandy. Chill for a few minutes."

She seemed relieved, which was what he was after. She gripped her crutches and headed toward the couch. An odd thought struck. What if he was attracted to Megan because she was in a cast?

The idea stopped him in his tracks. Did he have a cast fetish, previously undetected? Was he actually turned on by her broken leg?

Nah. He couldn't be. There was that woman in arbitrage who'd had a cast. He hadn't thought anything of it, and she was an attractive blonde.

Relieved, he got his snifter. He almost went to sit next to her on the couch, but changed his mind at the last second. He took the chair across from her. She was sitting near the window, her crutches tucked neatly by the side of the couch. If she was surprised by his choice of seating, it took her a minute to settle in, her broken leg stretched out in front of her, mostly hidden by her long skirt.

He liked the way she looked in it, sort of innocent. Like something she'd wear to church. Her sweater mitigated the virginal qualities, molding to her breasts like that. The contrast worked. She'd done something different with her hair tonight, too, although he'd be hard-pressed to say what. It didn't matter. He liked looking at her, liked the way her head tilted slightly to the side. The way her full lips curled into a Mona Lisa smile. The longer he knew her, the more he noticed how pretty she was. Weird. Usually, just the opposite happened.

She held her snifter cupped between both her hands, and her gaze had locked on the fire.

He took a sip of brandy and settled into the overstuffed wing chair. Megan turned slowly toward him, as if he'd awakened her from a trance.

"You okay?"

She nodded. "More than okay. Tonight's been great."

"We're not even to the halfway point yet."

"I know. But still. You really surprise me."

"I do?"

"Yeah. You're..." She looked back at the fire. "You're more than I would have guessed."

"How so?"

"More of a gentleman. More funny. More considerate."

"I don't know. I'm just me. Nothing special."

Her gaze came back to meet his own. "On the contrary. You're very special. I'm glad we met."

"Me, too."

He wanted to kiss her. To touch her. But he stayed in his chair, content to watch her. She'd let him know when she was ready.

"What else do you love?" she asked.

He thought he understood the question, but he had no easy answer. "Taking things to the max," he said, finally.

"Explain."

"I really like to ski, but that's not what keeps me coming back. It's that when I'm skiing, I'm pushing myself as hard as possible. I'm going beyond what I think I can do. That's the real rush."

"That's a good thing to love. Not how you compare to others, but how you compare to your own image of yourself."

"Exactly. I try to do that with everything, but I'm not always successful."

"You mean at work?"

He half smiled. "I heard a corny saying once a long time ago. That life is a game and money is how you tell who's winning."

"You believe that?"

"Sometimes. Most of the time. I've been poor. There's nothing noble about it. It sucks."

"True. But what lengths are you willing to go to so that you're not poor?"

"Ah, ethics."

"Yeah, those." She held his gaze, her eyes serious.

"I'm not willing to cheat my clients. I won't lie to them."

"So then being honest is more important than money."

"I hadn't thought about it, but yes. I think that's right. There have been times in my life when all I've had is my word. It matters."

She looked at him for a long moment, then she looked down at her leg. He thought she was going to say something, but she didn't. Not for a long time.

Had he said something wrong? The connection he'd felt all night wasn't there any more. He wanted it back. "Truth or dare," he said.

She looked at him, tried to smile, but didn't quite succeed. "I don't know if I—"

"Hey, no fair chickening out. Truth or dare?"

She nibbled her bottom lip for a second. Then she took a swig of brandy and when she looked at him again, she was smiling. Whatever had tripped her up seemed gone now. Maybe it hadn't been there in the first place.

"Dare," she said.

He hadn't expected that. The way she'd been talking. Shit. He had no idea what to dare her.

"Hold on," he said. "Don't go away. I'll be right back." He headed for the bathroom. He needed time to consider his next move.

Megan watched him as he crossed the room. His shoulders were remarkably wide. Or maybe it was just that his waist was so trim. Who cared. It worked. Big time.

He went out of her range, and she sighed as she leaned back. She'd almost told him. Another minute and she probably would have. She wanted to tell him. But she couldn't find the right words. The first part was easy... "I've got a confession to make." The tricky part came after that. "I really didn't break my leg? I'm crippled, and this is just my way of fitting in?" It sounded terrible. She'd tried to make it funny, charming, anything but what it was. No luck. Especially after that little honesty discussion.

Thank goodness this was only a vacation fling. Her lie wouldn't matter in the long run. She'd never see him again, so what was the harm? She deserved this, dammit. A week, one lousy week, was all she asked for.

What really got her was that she's the one who'd shifted the conversation. Not to mention the fact that she'd spooked him into sitting across the room.

Just a few moments ago, she'd been so pleased with herself for her honesty. See where it got her? Him on the chair, her on the couch.

Well, screw this. She wanted a night to remember. A scorching wicked night that would make her blush whenever she thought about it. This was a time-out. Not the real world. Not really her. She wanted her Man to Do.

The bathroom door opened, and she took another large sip of brandy. It burned, and she coughed a bit, but then she felt the edges blur, and everything was going to be just fine.

Luke went straight to the chair, and she felt a kick of disappointment. Until she saw his expression, that is. Oh, my. This was going to be some dare.

"You ready?"

"I think so. I'm not sure."

"Be sure," he said, his voice roughened, like it had been last night in bed.

She nodded even as her muscles tightened and her tummy clenched.

"Remember," he said. "You chose dare."

She stared at him, waiting. Her heart going a hundred miles an hour.

"I dare you to lift your skirt. All the way up. Then take off your panties and toss them over here."

12
___

AND SHE'D BEEN embarrassed when he'd touched her under the table.

"Uh, Luke…"

"You chose dare."

"What the hell was I thinking?"

He laughed, but he didn't take the dare back. "Tick-tock."

"Okay, okay. Jeez." She tried to figure out a way to carry out his instructions that wouldn't make her want to crawl under the couch cushions, but nothing came to her. She cursed herself for that debauchery comment. On the other hand, the whole purpose of tonight was sex. Hot, wild, uninhibited sex. Only, she'd forgotten to change her personality before dinner.

But, fair was fair. She took another swig of brandy and shivered as it went down. Then she took hold of her skirt and started pulling it up. Slowly. Real slowly.

His gaze was rapt as he watched the progress. She focused strictly on him, on the hunger in his eyes. By the time her skirt got above her knees, she didn't feel so embarrassed anymore. He wanted her. Was entranced by this little show, and the feeling was heady and dangerous.

No one had ever looked at her this way before. Not Jeff, not anyone. She toyed with him, spreading her legs, inching the skirt up, pausing. Then she got brave.

She ran her fingers up her thighs, under the skirt. When she hit her panties, she teased herself, mimicking his movements. Going even farther. Slipping her fingers inside the silk panties, until she felt her own damp flesh, until she found the already hardened bud. Never closing her eyes, she rubbed, increasing her tempo as her pleasure center reacted.

Luke's gaze lifted until it met her own, and she nearly came just looking at him. His eyes had dilated, his focus was so intense there seemed to be nothing else in the world except him and her and the sensations coursing through her body.

She tensed, trembled with the beginnings of an orgasm. Luke leaned forward, arching toward her as if he was going to leap off the chair any second.

With all the willpower she had ever had, she waited until his lips parted and he gripped the arms of his chair, and then she stopped. Just stopped.

She retraced her inner thighs. Took hold of her skirt once more. Pulled the material up another inch. And got her brandy snifter from the end table.

Luke's face had reddened quite a bit. His eyes got really wide, too. She chuckled, loving it. He might have offered the dare, but she'd raised the stakes. Incredible what she could do when she let herself go.

"No fair," he said. "That wasn't the dare."

"I'm not finished."

"But—"

''What's the matter?'' she asked. ''Is it too warm over there by the fire?''

''Cute. Frustrating as hell, but cute.''

''Thanks. I thought you might like it.''

''I'd like it better if you weren't such a tease.''

She narrowed her eyes; looked at him coyly. ''I don't believe that for a minute.''

''How can you say that? I'm dying here.''

''I haven't known you long, but I'm quite certain you get off on the chase. That if things come too easily, you get bored. Whether it's stocks, or skiing or women. Right?''

His brows came down as he settled back in his chair. ''Hmm.''

''Yes?''

''You're right. I do get bored easily. However, and I can't emphasize this enough, I'm not bored now. I haven't been bored since I met you.''

''Oh, how sweet.''

''Screw sweet. Take off your panties.''

She laughed. ''About that. There's a little problem.''

''What?''

''Logistics. I can lift my skirt up. I can spread my legs. But I can't take my panties off.''

''Why not? Are they glued on?''

''No. But, see, I have this broken leg. In a cast.''

He closed his eyes for a moment. ''Shit.'' He opened them again, his cheeks even redder than a moment ago. ''I didn't think it through.''

''Yeah. I figured.''

''There's a solution, you know.''

''And what would that be?''

He stood, walked over to the couch, grabbed her beneath her knees and behind her back, and lifted her into his arms. She thought he was going to the bedroom in a repeat of last night's entertainment, but he went to the wet bar instead. He put her gently on the counter, on a towel. She opened her mouth to ask him what he was doing, but his lips came down on hers. Hungry, demanding. He plunged his tongue inside her as if it was her sex. She gasped, grabbed his shoulders and hung on.

He nestled between her legs and with no teasing at all lifted her skirt up until it met the edge of the counter. "Lift up," he whispered.

She balanced her hands on the counter and when she had cleared the way, he pulled the material all the way up in back of her. When she sat again, it was on the towel, the nubs tickling the edges of her thighs.

He kissed her again, hard and fast. Then he grabbed her panties, and tugged. She heard the tear before she felt it. A second later, and she was naked from the waist down.

His fingers found her again, dipping inside her with equal parts urgency and care. She arched, stunned at the intensity of her reaction, her whole body electrified.

"Oh, God," he whispered against her lips. "Megan."

She moaned when he kissed her neck. Nibbled just beneath her ear. She cried out when he knelt down, spread her legs with burning hands and slipped his hot, hard tongue between her nether lips.

Her head lolled back, her eyes closed and she

sailed on a sea of ecstasy. He played her as if she
were an instrument, as if he were a maestro.

"Oh, God," she whispered, more to herself than
him. "This is... I can't... Oh, God."

He did things she'd never felt before, hard, soft,
nipping, sucking, all manner of delights with one purpose. To push her off the edge of the cliff, to let her
fall in space as one spasm followed another and another, until she keened and grabbed his hair, and
forced him to stop before she died of bliss.

He stood quickly, and as she caught her breath, he
undressed. Tossing his shirt behind him, he pulled a
gold packet from his pocket, then unzipped his jeans
and pulled them down, kicking them to the side.

Naked, gorgeous, hard as steel with a pearl of
moisture on the end of his cock, he put the condom
on, then came at her again. Grasping her around her
hips, he pulled her forward until she was at the very
edge of the counter. Without pause, he thrust inside
her, filling her, making her gasp. She was so sensitive
that she came again, and he groaned as her muscles
tightened, holding him in her sheath.

He pulled out slowly, then thrust in again, the en-
tire considerable length of him. Megan held on to
him by the shoulders, tense muscles bulging and flex-
ing beneath her hands. He captured her in another
kiss, and she tasted herself on this lips, his tongue.

He kept up a steady rhythm, pounding into her.
She felt like a wild animal, rough and strong and
feral.

He released her mouth, closed his eyes. The pace
quickened, and he grimaced, the cords of his neck
straining. She felt him swell, knew he was seconds

from his climax. She squeezed her internal muscles, and that was it. He came with a primal roar that thrilled her in a way she could hardly understand.

For a long moment he was very still, panting as if he'd run a fast mile. She panted, too, the energy draining from her as she fought for equilibrium.

"Wow," he said.

"I know."

"Did your leg bother you?"

She shook her head. "What leg?"

"Cool."

"I concur. Definitely one for the paper. Perhaps you should mention that the subject was pleased. Very, very pleased."

He grinned. "Really?"

"Uh, yeah."

"Always happy to be of assistance in your orgasmic needs."

"Ditto."

"I need liquid," he said. "Nonalcoholic, thirst-quenching."

"Mmm. Sounds perfect."

"You okay there?"

"For the moment."

He kissed her as he pulled out. By the time she opened her eyes, he was gone, in the bathroom, she presumed. She settled her skirt over her legs, self-conscious once again now that her lust was sated.

She leaned back, braced by her arms. What an unbelievable night. It was by far the hottest sexual encounter she'd ever had. Not just the technical aspects, either. The chemistry she felt with Luke totally blew her away. She hadn't even been like this with her fiancé.

The thought that she wouldn't see Luke again unsettled her. Just today, she'd counted that as a blessing. Now, it filled her with sadness. Was she that hard up for good sex?

Yeah, she was. But this wasn't just about sex. She wasn't sure what was going on, only that she didn't want tonight to end. She didn't want to go back to work. Mostly, she didn't want to say goodbye to Luke.

He came back into the living room wearing a white robe. He kissed her, tasting minty fresh. Then she was in his arms again, being carried like some kind of fairy-tale princess. He took her to the bedroom, and set her down.

"I've got water, soda, juice. What can I get you?"

"Water, please."

"Be back in a minute. You can get out of that sweater if you want."

"I can, huh?"

"Well, at least one of us hopes you will."

She felt her cheeks warm. He sure knew what to say.

He left her in the bedroom, and she undressed, tossing her sweater, bra and skirt on the chair by the wall. It wasn't easy pulling the covers over her with the damn cast on, but she managed. As she leaned back against the pillows, Luke arrived with her water. He put it on the nightstand, then jumped over her, to land with a thud on his side of the bed.

"I was thinking," he said.

"Oh?"

"Yeah. You have four days left, right? So, if you're not otherwise occupied... I mean, we're just getting started with the experiments and all."

Oh, my. Megan masked her reaction by getting her water glass, but inside she was flipping out. He wanted to see her again. She'd never dared hope. Damn, wait till she told June. Maybe he wasn't just a Man To Do. Maybe he was a Man To Keep. A Man to—

The lie. How could she have forgotten, even for a second. He could never be a Man To Keep. She'd boxed herself into a tight little corner, and that was that. No escape clause. Not a one. But that didn't mean she couldn't enjoy the rest of her vacation. "I think something could be arranged," she said, putting her glass back down, struggling to focus on the here and now.

"Excellent. So I guess I don't have to pull out all my best moves tonight, huh? I can save a little for tomorrow?"

"Those weren't all your best moves?"

He grinned in that way he had, that mischievous, sexy way. "Heck, no. Tonight was just an appetizer. The main course hasn't been served yet."

She blinked. "So much for catching up on my reading."

"You can read. During the day. But at night, you're mine."

She grinned happily and snuggled down in the bed. Luke tossed his robe aside and joined her. He wrapped his leg over hers, pulled her tight against his side. She sighed, loving the closeness, the feel of his hard body. She wouldn't think about going home.

She didn't want one thing to spoil the most special week of her life.

This is what she'd remember. This closeness. Feeling part of something bigger than herself. Being alone was fine and all, but damn, being with someone, someone you could count on, who was completely into the relationship—or the pretense, whichever came first—was amazing.

Megan closed her eyes and tried to imagine what it would be like to love someone who loved her back. To have that love be real and substantial, just like in the vows. For better or worse, in sickness and health, even with a crippled leg. That kind of love would change everything.

She felt his soft breath on the side of her neck, his hand resting softly on her breast. He'd fallen asleep. She'd thought she'd be the first one to conk out, but dreams of an unattainable future held her awake.

Imagine being with someone who cared about her day. Who believed in her work. Someone who would make Valentine's Day worth celebrating, instead of the torturefest she wallowed in with her other single friends.

And New Years! Oh, man. To be in Luke's arms at the countdown, and when the clock struck midnight, they would kiss and she wouldn't hear the shouts or the fireworks because she would be his—

She scrunched her eyes, willing herself to stop. She'd gotten what she asked for, so what was her problem? Hell, she'd gotten so much more than she could have ever hoped for! Luke was the most perfect Man To Do in the world. He'd proven her theory, which had a good side and a bad.

So now she knew. It was the leg. Not her personality, her hair, her face. The leg set her apart, and it was no use wishing and hoping it wasn't the case. Maybe now, with the truth in front of her, she could give up her crazy dreams, and settle into her real destiny. Go out with one of those dorky guys that gravitated to her. Find someone with a good sense of humor. That was important.

So it wouldn't be Luke.

At least she'd had these few days. It would be enough. It had to be.

MEGAN COULDN'T believe it. The week was almost over. Her last night had come too fast. Heartbreakingly fast.

Luke had skied his three days away while she'd drawn, did her e-mail, slept, slept some more, pampered herself, was pampered by others...the dreamiest, most heavenly three days of her life. But they'd been nothing compared to the nights.

True to his word, Luke had come up with incredibly inventive ways to overcome the obstacle of her cast. Standing, with her leaning against the shower wall. Sitting on a chair, on the couch, her on top, him on his side. She actually did think they qualified for a world record of some sort.

But the truly weird thing was, the sex wasn't the best part.

She looked over at Luke, sound asleep after another marathon, breathtaking lovemaking session. It was so tempting to let herself get depressed. She didn't want to leave. She'd give anything to stay with this amazing man.

How they'd talked. Long into the wee hours, about everything. Hopes and dreams, fears and sadness. She only wished she could have talked to him about the accident. About her leg. He was so understanding about everything else.

But it wasn't meant to be. He'd mapped out his life for her, his blessed master plan. It was clear he wasn't going to change that, not for anyone. She had to admire him for his discipline. There was no doubt he'd make his goals, live the life he dreamed of. A life of sports, outdoor activities, pushing himself past his limits. Not a very welcoming atmosphere for someone with a disability. He needed to find himself a woman who could keep up with him. Not her.

At least she'd had this week. Everyone in her on-line group had said the same thing—that she was incredibly lucky to have had her dream come true. Not just that she'd hooked up with Luke, but that she'd let herself be brazen and bold. She'd grabbed hold of life with both hands, and ridden until she was worn out. That was something, wasn't it?

Maybe she could take back some of this newfound bravura, stand up to Damian a little more, pursue her design goals with the same kind of determination she saw in Luke.

If only…

No. Not again. So she liked herself better when she was with Luke. The attitude shift didn't have to stop when they said goodbye. She'd remember him. His courage, his stamina, his focus, and she'd make changes. Substantial changes that would make him a part of her life forever.

He snorted, turned over, exposing his strong shoulder and magnificent back. He'd been amazing, staying up as late as they had then skiing like an Olympic athlete. She'd given him plenty of opportunities to take the evening off, get to bed early. But he'd laughed off the suggestion. Insatiable. That's what he was. Oh, yeah.

She snuggled down in his bed, pressing her good leg against him. Running her hand down his side. She closed her eyes, and said a silent "thank you" for this gift. He'd changed her. Forever.

LUKE WOKE UP with his arms around Megan. She fit perfectly in the curve of his body, and her soft warmth made him want to stay in bed forever.

She looked so beautiful. Her hair was a wild mess on the pillow, she had mascara smudges below her eyes and she was snoring. A cute snore, but a snore nonetheless. Oddly, it didn't bother him. Usually, he got turned off by a woman snoring. A lot of things were different with Megan.

Mostly, how he felt being with her. She made him laugh. A lot. That was right up there in his hit parade. He could clown around with her, and she didn't get all bent out of shape. She'd been a damn good sport, that's for sure.

It would have been a blast to be on the slopes with her. Stupid broken leg. Maybe next time, they could hit the slopes together.

Shit, what was he thinking? There wasn't going to be a next time.

He turned over to get a look at the clock. He'd blown his chance of ravaging her in the middle of the night. But maybe, if it wasn't too late, he could—

Nope. It was eight-forty-five, and he needed to get out there, do what he came here to do. She was leaving this afternoon, anyway, which was for the best, even if it didn't feel that way.

Moving carefully so he wouldn't wake her, he eased himself out of bed and found his bathrobe. As he looped the belt, his gaze moved back to Megan. The cast offset her small frame, and he wished he could see her without it. Oh, well.

He went to the bathroom, turned on the water so it would get hot while he brushed his teeth. Once he'd finished at the sink, he stepped inside the roomy shower and let the heat work its magic on his shoulders and back. His right arm ached, and so did his knee. He rubbed his bruises, and massaged his muscles as well as he could. Maybe he'd schedule a rubdown later. Give himself over to the spa masseuse. He'd been a jerk to keep the hours he had this week. It made him prone to injury, and that wasn't like him. Of course, nothing this week had been like him. Megan. Every night. And now that it was over, he didn't want it to end.

It had to, though. So he'd better get used to it.

He shampooed, shaved, washed, all in a matter of minutes as he'd learned to do on the road. When six guys shared one bathroom, time was of the essence.

Man, he'd been happy then. Before the accident. He'd been so damn sure he'd make the Olympic team. And so crushed when he hadn't.

But it was all for the best. If he had gone on to win a medal, he probably wouldn't have come up with the plan. And the plan was everything. It's what set him apart from the others. He felt like the ant in that old fable. The one who carefully prepared for winter, while his grasshopper buddy screwed around. He knew a hell of a lot of grasshoppers. They all rode him about it, but he'd be the one to have the last laugh. They wouldn't think it was so funny when he was living out his golden years in his condo in Vail, or Park City.

Which was just another reason it was good that Megan was going home. She was dangerous, that one. She made him waver, and dammit, wavering was unacceptable.

He turned off the water, and grabbed a towel from the rack. He'd get dressed in the living room. He didn't want her to wake up. It would make things too difficult. He'd leave her a note. A long one. A nice one. He'd tell her how much the week had meant to him. How great it was to have known her. He wouldn't wake her. If he did, he'd be tempted to ask her to stay. Or worse, he might ask to see her in the city.

No regrets. He didn't have room for regrets.

13

MEGAN WOKE to a shaft of sunlight in her eyes and an empty bed. She stretched languidly, then put her hand on Luke's pillow, in the depression left by his head. It was as cool as the room itself. She figured she'd put on some clothes while he was occupied, and check herself out in her compact. The raccoon look was highly overrated.

Humming a tune from Passion, she hobbled over to her overnight bag and pulled out the oversized T-shirt she'd intended to sleep in. Ha! As if. But it would do until she could shower and dress.

The compact showed the horror of her postsleep makeup, and while her fingers removed the worst of it, she needed to do the full washing routine before she'd look halfway human again.

She got her bag and made her way to the bathroom, ungainly and awkward being the operative words, expecting to find Luke inside. He wasn't.

Her stomach clenched. She wasn't sure how, but she knew as sure as the sun had risen that this wasn't good. When she saw the note taped to the mirror, her heart clenched, too.

Dear Megan,
I didn't want to wake you. You needed your rest

for your trip back home. I'm just sorry it all has
to come to an end. I've had the best damn time.
I mean it. You're an extraordinary woman, and
I'm so glad we got together. Maybe we'll meet
again next year. You'll have your cast off and
we can ski together. That would be great. In the
meantime, take care of yourself. And go for your
dreams! You'll have your own design company
before you know it. Be good but not too good.

Luke

There was no reason to cry. None at all. This was
her last day, and they'd both known it. Goodbyes
were always awkward and messy, and this made
things so much neater. But that didn't seem to matter
to the ache in her chest, or the lump in her throat.

He'd left her a goddamn note.

So much for fairy tales coming true.

She didn't want to shower here. She had to wash
up a bit, brush her hair, put on something, but that
was it, and she did it as fast as a crippled girl could.
Before she left, however, she called room service and
sent coffee to her room. She thought about charging
it to Luke, but she didn't.

She did leave him a note.

MEGAN GOT the whole back row to herself. The bus
was luxurious, which it damn well should have been
considering how much it cost. A few hours and she'd
be back in Manhattan, back in the real world. Alone.

In the meantime, she could catch up on her e-mail
for as long as her battery held out.

She took one last look at the lodge. It was truly

beautiful with icicles hanging from the eaves, incredible snow-capped mountains as the backdrop. Luke was on one of those mountains.

She whispered, "Goodbye," then turned to face the front of the bus. Her future. Her life.

The bus started moving, and she pulled out her laptop. Flipping it on, she went right to her e-mail. She'd downloaded before she'd left, but she hadn't bothered to read any.

The first one was the digest from Eve's Apple.

I've met the most wonderful man!!! He's incredible. Oh, you guys, this experiment was the best idea ever. His name is Paul and he's a producer. A real live producer with films to his credit and everything! He's gorgeous, too. Over six feet, dark hair with just a touch of gray at the temples. I can't even tell you how wonderful he was last night.

We met at the juice bar at my gym. His hair was still damp from a shower, and he asked me if I knew of a good sushi place. We talked and talked and talked. Went for sushi, then back to his hotel. He's scouting locations. It was a night from heaven. But that's not the best part. He's picking me up in an hour. We're going to the movies and dinner. I'll let you know what happens. I think he's more than a Man To Do. At least, I hope so! Kisses!

Gretchen.

Megan liked Gretchen, even though she was sort of flaky. Still, she hoped it worked out with the producer. Funny, how they'd all said they wanted a Man To Do, but now that the experiment was well under way, most of the woman desperately wanted much more than to do a guy. They wanted to keep a guy. Herself included.

Why was it so easy for men to have women and toss them aside like used hankies? Why couldn't women do that? It would make life so much easier. There wasn't even a word for it. Playgirl wasn't at all like a playboy. Not even close. Come to think of it, the only words she could come up with were pejorative. Here they were in the twenty-first century, and the double standard still ruled.

Was it the social pressures that made women yearn for marriage and kids? Or was it the innate need for mating and reproducing that made the social pressures?

She didn't know. All she knew for sure was that she missed Luke something fierce. And that she didn't want to go back to the way things were. She wanted a magic wand, a genie in a lamp. Something, anything, that would make things different. Better. Perfect.

She sighed, and started typing her own update. About the experiment, about Luke, about the fact that a Man To Do was all well and good in theory. In practice, she wasn't sure. Perhaps she'd have been better off not playing at all.

LUKE GOT BACK to his room a little after five. He'd had a mediocre day on the slopes, and he blamed himself for it. He'd been preoccupied. With Megan. Again.

He'd thought about her at the oddest times. Like when he was halfway down the mountain and one wrong move could kill him. Smart. Real smart.

He got out of his ski clothes, tossing them in the corner to be picked up later when he gave a crap. As soon as he walked into the bathroom, he checked out his note taped to the mirror. Only it wasn't his.

Dear Luke,
Truth: I had a blast. You made my vacation fantastic. Dare: Don't leave all the good parts until after you retire. You never know…make this the best time of your life.

                                        Megan

He tugged the note down, crumpling it tight for a quick trip to the round file. He turned on the water and stepped in the shower. For once, the heat failed to soothe. His muscles seemed tighter than ever.

That would teach him to break his own rules. No second dates. No attachments. He understood only too well the danger of buying into Megan's philosophy. She wasn't the first to try to convince him his plan was all wrong. Damn near every friend of his had given it a shot at one time or another. But they didn't get it. They didn't see that the sacrifice would all be worth it in the end. They hadn't seen his father's eyes. How he'd been dead for years before he actually keeled over.

Megan was great, sure. But no woman was worth abandoning his plan.

Maybe he'd look up that blonde. Peggy. Yeah, that was her name. She was hot.

He attacked his washing like he attacked every other job. Fast, thorough, no slacking. By the time he'd stepped out of the shower, he'd stopped thinking about Megan. He finished up in the bathroom, then went to get dressed. His gaze caught on the remote control, and he flipped on the tube.

There was a game on, and he watched as he got dressed. A pretty damn good game, from the looks of it.

He plumped up his pillows, and lay back on the bed. When his stomach grumbled, he called down to room service and ordered himself dinner. He'd find the blonde tomorrow.

ARMED WITH HOT COCOA complete with marshmallow, Megan sat curled up on her old club chair. June was on the couch in pajamas, robe and bunny slippers.

"Call him."

"Excuse me?"

June shrugged. "Call him. Tell him you like him. That you want to go out."

"Oh, right. Like that would work."

"Why not?"

"First, he doesn't want to go out with me again. He made that really clear." Megan sipped some cocoa, finding it surprisingly unsatisfying. "He's got that cockamamie plan of his, and he doesn't do second dates."

"What do you call sleeping with you every night of his vacation?"

"Vacation sex. Not applicable. Second, he left me a note. How blind would a person have to be not to get that hint."

"So he hates goodbyes. No big deal."

"Have we forgotten the little detail about my leg? About the fact that I lied to him?"

"So tell him," June said. "Confess. What's the worst that can happen?"

"He'll never want to see me again."

"He already doesn't want to see you again."

Megan blinked. She loved June like a sister, but sometimes...

"I'm not kidding, Megan. You have absolutely nothing to lose."

"At least now I have some pretty nice memories, you know? That was the whole point? That I'd have these wonderful memories to comfort me in my old age."

"That's a crock and you know it. You can't sleep with memories. You can't laugh with them, or show them your drawings. Face it, girl, you wanted a miracle and you didn't get one."

"But I did. I got Luke. Even if it was just for a few days."

June sighed, pushed back her hair and rubbed her eyes. She didn't look all that wonderful. She wasn't sleeping well. Plagued by insomnia, June said she'd made peace with it, but when she went for weeks waking up after a couple of hours sleep, Megan couldn't help but worry. June refused to go to a doctor. She just kept taking melatonin, even though it didn't seem to work at all. So who was she to be handing out advice like Dr. Phil?

"Megan, my dear," June said. "I know you think this little experiment proves something about who you are, but it doesn't. It could just as easily have gone the other way. Bottom line, you have no idea if Luke would have done exactly the same thing if you hadn't had the cast.''

"Oh, please. That's so untrue. First of all, I wouldn't have been there.''

"Why not? People with disabilities ski all the time.''

"You honestly expect me to risk crippling my other leg? That would be swell. This building doesn't even have a ramp for a wheelchair.''

"Bull. You're just chicken. If you're careful, and you take lessons, you won't get hurt.''

"My mother was driving the speed limit. We had seat belts on.''

June sighed again. "Fine. Have it your way. But dammit, Megan, Luke may have been this wonderful guy, or maybe not. You don't know him well enough, and you haven't seen him in his true context. So don't make him out to be Prince Charming.''

"You have such confidence in me. It's touching.''

"When it comes to this, I don't. I think you're brilliant and beautiful and funny, and if I were a guy I'd marry you myself. But all you see is what's wrong with you, not what's right. You're more than your stupid leg.''

Megan uncurled her legs and stood up. She went to the couch and kissed June on the cheek. "I love you, girl. You're the best. I appreciate what you're saying.''

June looked up, her dark eyes sad and soulful. "But you don't believe me.''

"I try. Honestly, I do.''

"I guess that's all I can ask.''

Megan went to the kitchen, opened the fridge and

stared at the alarmingly bare shelves. Groceries tomorrow. "Hey, did Darlene say when she'd be back?"

"She wasn't sure. A few days. Four at the most."

"Damn, I can't wait to get this thing off. Do you think I could just cut it off?"

"I'd wait." June joined her at the fridge. "I know nothing about casts. I have no clue if you could do something bad by cutting it off yourself."

"I guess a few days won't kill me. People usually wear these things for six weeks."

"Where are you working tomorrow?"

Megan slammed the door shut. "Central Park."

"Cool."

"No, it's not. It's cold. Freezing. I can't wear gloves while I draw."

"Bummer."

"Indeed."

June checked her watch. "It's past my bedtime. I'm glad you're home."

Megan smiled. "Me, too."

"Don't despair, sweetie," June said, hitting her lightly on the shoulder. "Things change. Mysteries prevail. Wonders never cease."

"Go to bed, June. You're starting to sound like a greeting card."

"Humph. Some greeting cards are very poignant."

"Yeah, that's you, girl. Poignant as all get-out."

After a very unladylike raspberry, June let herself out. Megan was still hungry, but her only food choice seemed to be mac and cheese in the blue box, or spaghetti, which were both fine, but not at ten-thirty at night.

She poured herself a glass of water, and shuffled toward the bathroom, her clunky fuzzy slippers a half size too big, and always threatening to come off. She supposed it would be easier to buy a new pair, but she liked these. Although, using the crutches made it more precarious to walk much.

A few more days. That's all. Then she could go back to the brace. She wanted to do it sooner than that. She needed to accept the facts of her life. It would only delay the inevitable if she continued to pretend something wonderful was going to happen. Despite what June said, miracles rarely happened, wonders ceased all the time, and despair seemed particularly appropriate.

To bed. Tomorrow, work. Freezing fingers. Overheated subways. *Welcome to the real world. Yehaw.*

LUKE HUNG UP the phone and stared at his computer. He'd been back from vacation three days, and he was pretty much in the swing of things again. His stocks had done well while he'd been gone, and no one was in a panic. Politics being what they were, that could change in a heartbeat, but for now, all was calm. Well, as calm as Manhattan can be.

He'd scheduled lunch with his buddy Cal. Luke hadn't seen him in over a month, what with Cal changing jobs and stuff. They usually played racquetball in the mornings, and Luke was anxious to get back into the routine.

Cal was a good guy. Bright as hell. Worked for Morgan Stanley, made enough money to have bought a three-bedroom condo in the high-rent district in

Chelsea. The really good thing about him, though, was that he hated to talk about work.

There was still a half hour before he had to leave, so he clicked back to the Internet site he'd found this morning. Fashion design wasn't for sissies. It was hard as hell to break in, and the capitalization was damn high. But someone as talented as Megan should be able to do it.

There were some interesting grant situations, and some venture capitalists that might be of interest to her. He should have gotten her e-mail address. Or her phone number. Just to give her a hand, nothing more. A tip or two.

Shit, when was he going to get over this? He'd thought of her way too much since he'd been back. Nothing that spectacular had happened. Except for the sex. And the game. And talking. Ah, man. He was seriously in trouble here, and he needed to do something about it, fast.

First, he turned off his computer. Second, he got out his little black book, which happened to be brown leather, and flipped through the pages. He didn't have second dates, but he did have some bed buddies he knew were safe. Who wanted nothing more than sex, and lots of it.

Jessica. Ah, yes. Lovely Jess. She was tall, gorgeous and she could drink him under the table. He dialed her number and left her a message. Was she free? Tonight?

By the time he hung up, he had to leave. Cal would get his mind off Megan.

"WHAT HAPPENED TO YOU?"

Megan looked up at Stacey, the craft service

woman. They often talked when the company was on location. Stacey was great at setting up food for the crew. Just enough lettuce and endive to make the models happy, and just enough donuts and breakfast burritos to satisfy the teamsters. "Nothing bad. I'll have it off in a couple of days."

"It didn't wreck your vacation?"

She shook her head. "Nope. All's well. How are you?"

Stacey filled her in on her latest family drama. Her husband was an alcoholic who sometimes went to AA. Her son, Del, was following in dad's footsteps, even though he was only a sophomore in high school.

It felt good to listen to someone else's woes, although she was embarrassed to admit it. She was just so damn tired of feeling so blue. She hadn't known Luke long enough to be this sad.

She'd get the cast off tomorrow, and then things should settle down. At least she hoped they would.

Her gaze snapped onto a guy across the street, but it wasn't Luke. He had similar hair, that's all. It was nuts. She kept thinking she saw him. In a city this size, with so many millions of people, the likelihood of seeing Luke was about one in a gazillion. Yet she kept looking. Hoping.

"You okay?"

She snapped back to Stacey. "Yes, I'm fine. Just a little distracted. Postvacation blues, that's all."

"I understand. Sure. Hey, I've got a couple of Twinkies stashed in the truck. Want one?"

"Damn straight."

"I'll be right back."

Megan watched the flow of pedestrians as she waited. Every male who had anything even remotely in common with Luke got her attention. It was ludicrous.

It was over with him. He was gone. History. Yesterday's news. And she'd be skating on the river Styx before she'd hear from him again.

MEGAN ALMOST KILLED HERSELF rushing to the phone. It was late, and she was freezing, and she wanted nothing more than a bath and bed. What a day.

She grabbed the phone. It was a recorded message telling her she was preapproved for something she didn't want. Damn. Her machine blinked at her. She pressed the button, listening as she filled her teakettle with water.

"Megan? Hi. It's, ah, Luke. From skiing. I hope you don't mind that I called."

She dropped the kettle, splashed water all over the sink and herself and missed the rest of the message. With trembling hands, she pressed the button to listen again.

"...I was wondering if you'd like to have dinner tomorrow night. Or whenever. I've been doing some research on fashion design financing, and I thought we could talk about it."

He gave her his cell number, which she wrote down. Then she listened to the message about a hundred more times.

He'd called. Thank God she hadn't taken off the cast. She shouldn't see him. It was stupid and would only lead to more pain.

Yeah. Right.

14

SHE ENDED UP taking the answering machine into the bathroom, but her overall plan fell apart when she realized as soon as she pressed Play from the tub, she'd be electrocuted. So she made do with the memory of his voice, repeating his words over and over as she tried to get comfortable.

Having to stick her leg out of the tub diminished the experience of the bath by a lot. It probably would have upset her if she wasn't on cloud nine.

He wanted to see her. He'd been thinking about her. He'd had to find her phone number, so that meant he remembered her last name. She plugged her nose and dipped beneath the water, and she didn't come back up until she couldn't stand it another second. Taking great, gasping gulps of air, she tried to be rational. Really tried.

It was no use. All her logic and reason, and especially her caution simply couldn't stand up to the amazing miracle that Luke Webster had actually called her back in the city!

While she couldn't use the answering machine from the tub, she could use her telephone. Unfortunately, June was out. Megan felt reasonably sure she'd call the minute she got in, having left her about a hundred messages.

Sure enough, just as she was soaping up the loofah, the phone rang.

"What the hell?"

"Are you sitting down?"

June grunted. "Yes."

"You are not."

"What difference does it make? And how did you know?"

"I hear you at the sink, you goof."

"So, tell me why you called eighty billion times."

Megan thought about being coy. Like that was gonna happen. "He called."

"By he, I'm assuming you mean Luke?"

"Yes, yes, yes, yes. He called. Me. On the phone."

"Okay, I think I'm beginning to get the picture. He called. You. On the phone."

"Yes. He wants to have dinner tomorrow."

"What happened to his master plan? No second dates? All that crap?"

"I guess he decided he'd break the rules for me. Ha!"

"Ha is right. Honey, have you forgotten something? Your relationship with Luke is based on a—"

"I know. Don't say it."

"My not saying it isn't going to change the facts."

"But he called. He wants to have dinner."

"I understand. Honestly, I do. And far be it from me to put roadblocks on the course of true love, but you're going to have to tell him the truth at some point. I mean, you can't wear the cast for the rest of your life."

"Do you really think we'll see each other a lot? I mean, into the future? Like for a month, or a year or something?"

"How would I know? All I'm saying is you're supposed to get your cast off tomorrow. I gather you're going to postpone it, but you can't wait too long. For all we know, your leg will rot and fall off."

"I don't think so. But I'll ask, okay?"

"Hey, it's your leg."

"I know, but jeez. Give me a break. The hottest man in the history of the world just asked me out. I'm a little stunned."

"Look, I'm happy for you. Honestly. I applaud the guy for seeing how incredible you are. I bet if you gave him half a chance, he'd come through for you. If he's that wonderful…"

"Stop. No more. I don't want to hear another word about the cast. Not tonight. Tonight is for basking."

"Fair enough. We won't speak of it again. We'll concentrate on the far more important topic of wardrobe decisions."

"I love you."

"I know you do. Now get out of the tub before you prune. I'm coming over as soon as I shove some food down my throat."

"Yes, ma'am."

LUKE CHECKED HIS WATCH. It was exactly thirty-two seconds later than the last time he'd looked. He felt like a teenager waiting for his prom date. Ridiculous.

All he wanted to do was go over some investment strategies with Megan. No biggie. She was nice, he believed in her talent, he had some expertise to share.

He'd be a jackass not to help her. And who knows, if she made it, she might turn to him as her financial advisor, so he was in fact looking out for his own best interests.

Not to mention the fact that he got hard just thinking about her.

Ah, man. He was blowing it. Big time. Even Cal, who rarely mentioned his own personal life let alone Luke's, had been startled about Megan. As Cal had so accurately pointed out, the master plan has been his whole life, his raison d'être. No woman, and there had been some hotties, had ever tempted him to veer off course.

A cab stopped in front of the restaurant, but it wasn't Megan. Luke shoved his hands in his pockets, and began to pace. He was the least romantic person he knew. Unsentimental to a fault. He'd trained himself to be vigilant and disciplined. Of course, he'd screwed up, he was human. But not when it came to the big stuff.

Who said this was big? Jeez. He was losing it. This was about finances, nothing more. Okay, finances and friendship. Nothing wrong with that. Hey, he needed people. He wasn't ashamed to admit that. He and Megan had clicked, that's all. Even ignoring the great sex, she was someone worth knowing. He felt at ease with her. Like they'd been friends for years.

He stopped. Stared at his reflection in the restaurant window. He'd worn his wool coat, his cashmere scarf and gloves. Underneath was the Dolce & Gabbana three-piece suit with one of the silk ties he'd bought in Switzerland. These weren't his work clothes, except for the coat. They were the clothes he wore when he wanted to impress.

Why did he want to impress Megan? If it had been another guy, would he have gone to the trouble? For Christ's sake, he had on Hugo Boss cologne.

His focus shifted to the pedestrians behind him. Everyone scurrying in their bulky coats, hats, scarves and mufflers hid everything but the attitude. Eyes forward, downcast. Shoulders hunched. Purses tucked away, backpacks locked, and the pace unrelentingly fast. Rushing from point A to point B in the shortest possible time, with the least amount of human interaction. Manhattan in all its winter glory. And dammit, he loved it. Loved the pace, the smells of every kind of ethnic food imaginable, the sound of horns and street musicians, the lights, the rumble of the subway beneath his feet. There were two places he truly felt alive. One was skiing down a giant slalom, the other was right here. In the heart of the city.

It was easy to stay focused here. Hell, everyone he knew was driven to make more money, get the promotion, buy the right co-op. It was a town filled with young Turks, and he was in the thick of it.

The trick was to keep himself as liquid as his investments. He had to be free to buy, to sell, to risk. He'd walked the tightrope plenty in the past eight years, and he seriously doubted he would have made the same decisions if he'd been married, or even had a serious relationship.

Karl Snedeger. God, he hadn't thought of him in a long time. He'd been a wunderkind, a genius on the Street. He'd made himself and his clients millionaires ten times over. And then he'd found Debbi, and that was the beginning of the end.

Within two years, he'd lost most of his client base, not to mention his own fortune. He'd never admit it was his infatuation that had steered him off the course, but everyone knew it.

Object lessons. The world was filled with them, if he'd just pay attention. Eyes on the prize. No detours. No complications. What part of that didn't he understand?

"Hi."

Luke saw her in the glass. Her shining smile, those incredible eyes. His heart slammed in his chest as if he'd just boosted ten feet out of a halfpipe. He turned around, and before he even said hello he had her in his arms, crutches and all. His lips found hers, startled by the cold. But growing warmer by the second.

She pulled back, but just a little. Just enough to whisper, "Hi."

"Hi."

They stood still for a long time, him wishing they weren't so dressed. Her smiling like she'd just been given a free trip to Paradise.

"I can't believe you called."

He shrugged. "Yeah, well, with you bugging me all the time to research funding options—"

"Hey."

He laughed. "We should probably go in. We don't want them to give away our reservation."

"Sure," she said.

But he didn't let her go just yet. Instead, he kissed her, and it felt so damn good.

BY THE TIME she'd finished her salad, which was a magic concoction of endive, candied walnuts and fib balsamico, Luke had given her more solid advice about her future than all the teachers at her college. She'd tried taking notes, but he'd put all the information on a disk for her. "I can't believe how much work you did on this," she said. "I don't know how to thank you."

His cocked eyebrow told her he had a few ideas.

She laughed. "No, I'm serious. I know this must have taken hours. It's not as if you have all this free time."

"It wasn't such a big sacrifice," he said. "It's all pretty straightforward if you know where to look."

"Regardless, I'm grateful. I actually think I've got a shot. If I've got the talent."

"You do. I still can't get over your drawings. I think you're going to be the next Donna Karan."

"From your lips." She looked up as the waiter brought their entrées. She'd ordered seared sea scallops with asparagus, black trumpet mushrooms and sweet onions. Luke had the crispy lemon chicken with glazed root vegetables and lemon herb spaetzle. Gorgeously presented, as much art as dinner. It was her first time at the bistro, although she'd read about it in *The New Yorker*. It was part of the rebuilding project in Tribeca, the concerted effort by so many in New York to bring life back to this end of the city after 9-11.

The tables were filled with trendy folks, many from the nearby financial district, and quite a few from the arts center that Robert DeNiro had pioneered in this little section of Manhattan. She recognized a photographer she'd worked with on a *Vogue* shoot, and there was a gaggle of models seated where they could get the best exposure and flattering light.

She turned to Luke. "What do you call a group of models?"

"A group?"

"You know. Like an exultation of larks. A murder of crows. A gaggle of geese."

"Ah," he said, grinning. "I'm not sure. Maybe an emaciation of models?"

"Good one. How about a gag?"

"Excellent." He lifted his wineglass. "It makes one think. What about stockbrokers?"

"Oh, interesting." She thought for a moment. "A panic of stockbrokers?"

His brows raised. "Brava."

She bowed. "Thank you."

"But we're not finished."

"No?"

"How about designers?"

"Ah. Designers. I think a conceit. Yes. A conceit of designers."

"You're not at all conceited."

"Give me time. I'll get there."

He laughed as they got down to the highly pleasant task of eating. She wanted it to last forever. Not the food itself, but the night, the ambiance, the way she felt. Just the look in his eyes warmed her more than her big old coat.

It was so easy, being with him. She'd been fascinated watching him talk finance. His excitement was contagious. She'd learned early that the best way to fall in love with any subject was to talk with someone passionate about it. Not surprising, given the way he attacked his life. The skiing, the master plan...

Part of her bubble burst when she thought of that, and it took her a minute to let her fears go. June was right. She had to take the cast off sometime. Luke would get suspicious, eventually. And it was inconvenient as all get out at work. The crutches tripped everyone around her, no matter how hard she worked at tucking them away. It took her twice as long to walk anywhere.

Her boss was used to her brace, but he didn't like the idea of the cast. Too obvious, was her guess. Such a blatant sign of imperfection.

Screw him. The cast could stay another week with no harm. Maybe two. With any luck at all, a month. She had to make it last. Had to. How could she give up the best thing that had ever happened to her?

"Hey, what's up? Why so serious?"

She smiled, banishing all negative thoughts for the remainder of her time with Luke. "Nothing. Work." She waved her hand, dismissing the subject.

"No, ma'am. I'm not buying it."

"Pardon?"

"That look wasn't for nothing. Something's wrong. Come on, Megan. Truth."

She put her fork down as she considered just coming out and telling him the truth. What if June was right, and he was cool about it? Understanding?

On the other hand, nothing in her experience led her to believe this would all end up with a laugh and a hug. "It's really nothing. It was a tough day today, and my boss was on the rampage. He can be such a bitch when he wants to.''

"Tell me,'' Luke said, and he seemed to mean it.

"Really? You want to hear about the petty squabbles and temper tantrums of a prima donna fashion designer.''

"Sure. It involves you, doesn't it.''

She had to gulp in some air on that one because he'd quite simply taken her breath away. "Yeah, it does.''

"Then lay it out. I've always been curious about what happens on one of those high-fashion shoots.''

"It's not nearly as glamorous as one would be led to believe. In fact, it's mostly uncomfortable, with eons of downtime, waiting for this or that. Either the lighting isn't right or the model is crazy. Sometimes both at the same time.''

He nodded as he ate, maintaining eye contact, listening carefully. She talked and nibbled, and laughed and listened. They were both *there*. Really there.

The last guy she'd gone out with hadn't listened at all. He'd just waited for his turn to talk. Mostly about his rotten stepfather. Megan had been bored out of her mind.

With Luke, it was…

She didn't even have words. It was more than magic. It was bliss.

By the time he'd commiserated about how infuriating Damian was, and he'd filled her in on the gems he worked with, it was late. Almost midnight.

The restaurant was still reasonably full, so she didn't feel any urgency to leave, despite the fact she had a hideously early call tomorrow morning. She'd sleep later. She was going to hang on here as long as she could.

The waiter came by with a tray of the most decadent-looking desserts she'd ever seen. Great, squiggly lines of chocolate with tiny fruits and crème fraîche decorating a vanilla bean custard, next to a sinfully rich-looking mocha mousse. Of course they had crème brûlée, which caught her attention and held it. She shouldn't. Really.

"The lady will have the brûlée," Luke said. "And coffee. I'll have the napoleon. Coffee for me, too, please."

"Very good, sir," the waiter said, tugging at his monogrammed sleeves before he whisked the cart away.

"You realize I'm going to have to eat nothing but lettuce for a week after this meal."

"Don't. I love that you eat like a real person."

"What does that mean?"

"Do you know how many women I've gone out with who eat barely enough to keep a parakeet alive?"

"That's just for show. You do realize they go home and polish off a pint of Ben & Jerry's before they attack the Sara Lee, right?"

"I suspected such a thing, but since I've never actually witnessed it—"

"Trust me. Women are not the delicate flowers they'd like you to believe."

"Damn it. Why'd you have to go and spoil things for me."

"Someone had to tell you, Luke. I'm just sorry it had to be me."

He leaned forward and touched her hand. "I'm not. I'm very glad it's you."

She didn't quite trust herself to speak, so she just smiled.

"And just so we're clear, I haven't forgotten my research project. Millions are depending on my results, you know."

"Ah, the humanitarian effort."

He nodded. "How much longer are you going to be in the cast?"

She looked away as if to search for the waiter while she schooled her expression. "I'm not sure. I have to speak to the doctor."

"You're not getting it off before the weekend, are you?"

"I don't think so."

"Good." He jerked back a little. "That didn't come out right. Of course I want you to get the cast off. It must be uncomfortable as hell. Besides, outside of me and my noble efforts, what fun can you have with a bum leg?"

"Not much," she said.

15

THE CAB DOOR was open, and Megan adjusted her skirt while Luke put her crutches on the floorboard. It was impossibly late, after two, and they were both going to pay dearly for lingering so long. She'd tried to end the evening several times, but she just couldn't. She'd thought about asking him back to her apartment, but that seemed too far, too fast.

This wasn't vacation reality anymore, and the rules, at least most of them, came back into play. Odd that she was a little nervous about sleeping with him. Excited, but nervous.

She'd get over it.

"I'm sorry I kept you out so late," he said, leaning over, bracing himself on the cab roof and door. "Don't hate me too much in the morning."

"I won't hate you at all. I had the best time."

His smile, warm, intimate, made her want to get right out of the taxi.

"I did, too. Damn, girl. What am I going to do about this?"

"About what?"

Before he could answer the cabbie cleared his throat loudly and turned around. "If youse two are gonna talk, I gotta flip the meter."

"Go ahead," Luke said. "I won't be long."

The cabbie shrugged. He looked as though he'd seen it all and heard it twice. With his scraggly beard and the toothpick dangling from his lips, he looked like the guy that lived across the hall from her. The guy who propositioned her about once a month. It was hard to resist his charming, "Hey, you want to do it?"

"I'm not kidding," Luke said. "I really don't know what to do here."

"I don't fit into your plans, do I?"

He shook his head.

"For what it's worth, you don't fit into mine either. But that's okay. I'm all in favor of taking things one day at a time. Who knows what's going to happen tomorrow. I could be hit by a car."

He leaned over and kissed her gently on the lips. "Don't do that."

"I'll try not to."

He looked her in the eyes, his gaze steady and penetrating. "You'd better go now."

She didn't say anything. She couldn't.

Luke was the one to break the connection. He blinked. Pulled back. "Go home. Go to sleep. I'll call you."

"Okay. Thank you."

He nodded, smiled. Instead of shutting the door, however, he got his wallet from his pants pocket and gave the driver money.

"Hey, you don't have to do that. I can—"

"I know you can. But I wanted to." He closed the door then stepped back. "I'll call you."

"Okay," she said, just as the cabbie pulled out

into the street. She stared back at Luke until they turned on Greenwich.

"You want to tell me where we're going?"

She gave the driver her address, then leaned back on the seat, staring blindly at the dense buildings whipping past. At this time in the morning, the streets were pretty quiet. Some all-night stores were open, and of course after-hours clubs and bars. A mixture of trendy revelers and street people prowled for the currency of the night: sex, drugs, booze, mystery, anonymity. No place on earth was better equipped to fill the bill.

She closed her eyes and thought about her night. What was she searching for? Sex? Love? Hope?

It was too late to think about the mess she'd made. Instead, she pictured the feel of his lips on hers, and in a dreamy haze, she rode to her apartment. It was two-fifteen by the time she got there, and after three by the time her tired body said enough, and she slept.

LUKE MANAGED to make his morning workout, even though he'd only gotten about four hours of sleep. At the gym, just two blocks from the office, he skipped the weights and settled in on the treadmill. He'd do a few miles and hope that by the time he showered and headed to work, he'd be alert for the day.

He'd lain awake for a long time last night, thinking about Megan. He'd given up kidding himself that he wasn't going to call her again.

This whole situation was completely unprecedented. He'd never felt this way about a woman, and he wasn't happy about it.

Somehow, he had to figure out a way to see Megan and stick with his plan. It wasn't that many years until he could give up the job, get a summer place in the country. Have the life he'd always dreamed of. He'd buy a boat. Fish in the spring, ski in the winter. Did Megan like to fish? He'd ask her.

"Yo, Luke, my man. How's it hanging?"

Luke turned to the treadmill next to him. Benny, a personal trainer he'd used on several occasions was adjusting the controls to start his own workout.

"It's hanging pretty low, Benny," he said. "I'm running on fumes."

"You're in the right place to pick up some energy, buddy boy."

Benny started out at a stately pace, getting his blood working. The man was his own walking billboard with a six-pack worthy of Arnold Schwarzenegger. He was a good trainer, too. He'd helped Luke through a serious ligament problem.

"Let me ask you something." Luke increased the inclination on the treadmill. "You think it's possible to have a relationship with a woman without losing your edge as a trainer?"

"Why, you thinking of becoming my competition?"

"You know what I'm talking about. You've competed. Had to sacrifice for your goals."

"Yeah. But I was never one of those bozos who thought saving myself was going to give me an edge. Hell, I always work out better after a night of pumping the love muscle."

Luke grinned. "I'm not talking about sex. I'm talking about a relationship. Being involved."

"I don't know," Benny said. "I'm too damn pretty to let one woman have me. It would be selfish."

"Right. Come on. I'm serious here."

"Why, there some chick you're thinking about?"

"Yeah. In fact, she broke her leg in a skiing accident. I was thinking you might help her out once she gets the cast off."

"Bring her on."

"Thanks."

"Didn't think I'd ever see you fall."

"Me, neither."

Benny punched some buttons on his treadmill increasing his pace and the angle. When he was satisfied, he turned to Luke. "What's she got, this babe? Aside from a broken leg?"

"I don't know. She's just... Shit. I can't figure it out myself. I like her, that's all. I feel better when I'm with her."

"Whoa."

"You can say that again."

"So, try it. What's the worst that could happen? That's what I tell my clients. You gotta look at the big picture. You screw up, you get right back on track. It's the long haul that matters. If it don't work out with her, you cut your losses."

"What if it does work out?"

"Today, you felt shitty, but you came to work out, right?"

"Yeah."

"So, you do the same thing. Be with the babe, but keep on with the program. Don't change your routine. Add her into it."

Luke thought about it for a moment. What was it, exactly, about the master plan that precluded a relationship? The expense was one. But Megan didn't seem like the type to care much about that. She'd said herself she would be satisfied with hot dogs instead of lobster. He wasn't going to support her or anything like that. At least not for a long damn time.

What worried him more than the money issue was the focus. He credited his success in school, in skiing and now in the market to his one hundred percent commitment to excellence. He didn't let anything get in the way. All the parties he'd missed in college were worth it. He'd kept up his grades and his scholarship, which meant he didn't have to pay back a load of student loans. He'd nearly made it to the Olympics, and that's because he'd trained his ass off. Every day. It didn't matter what the weather was, or how he felt. He just did it.

He'd approached his job the same way. He kept himself fit, he didn't screw around or participate in all that office gossip garbage. He had a routine, he did his homework, and his clients stuck with him. They knew he was someone they could count on.

Would he still be that dedicated if Megan became part of his life?

"Hey, Luke."

"Yeah, Benny?"

"This babe… She got a sister?"

He laughed. "Sorry. She's one of a kind."

"Hell, man. This life is short. Didn't you learn that from 9-11? You better take the gifts God gives you, and be grateful for 'em. You found a keeper, then you do just that."

"Benny, you missed your calling. You should have been a psychiatrist, not a trainer."

"Screw that. I get paid more."

MEGAN FINISHED reading her e-mail and checked to make sure Damian was still talking to the art director. She had found a nice quiet corner where she could see what was up without getting sucked into any conversations. The morning had been pretty brutal. She'd woken so late she'd had to take a cab to work. Then Damian had been on the warpath. Seems a couple of rolls of film had been destroyed at the lab, and he had to go back to Coney Island to shoot there again. She didn't care. She'd done some good work this morning, and even though she could tell he wanted to bitch at her, he couldn't find anything wrong. That didn't happen very often. He'd looked at her funny, too, as if he could tell something was different. What he didn't know was that everything was different.

She was inspired. More than inspired.

The e-mails had been coming hot and heavy over the past few days. Two more of the Eve's Apple gang had hooked up with Men To Do. Eileen, who at forty-four was the oldest of the group, had done the Mrs. Robinson thing with a young stud she'd met at her art class. She was thrilled with the experience, although she'd assured them all that she didn't want to say "I do" ever again. However, after her night with Roger, she was all in favor of continuing to find Men To Do just for the hell of it.

Heather, who was a student at UCLA, and gay, had seduced a woman she'd met at a singles' bar. It had been the first time she'd ever done the initiating and she felt like a sex goddess.

Megan sipped some hot cocoa she'd picked up at the craft service table, then started her own e-mail.

Dear Everyone,

First, let me congratulate Eileen and Heather. Well done, ladies! You guys are too extraordinary for words. I'm awed.

Gretchen? Where are you? How goes it with your producer? Still walking on air?

As for me...

I've gotten myself into something of a pickle. A big, hairy dill pickle.

Luke called.

We went out.

It was heaven.

He still doesn't know about my leg, which is still in a cast. Which can't stay in a cast forever because, well, it just can't. But I don't want to take it off, because that would spoil everything, and oh, my God, it's much worse than I could ever have believed because, dammit, I've gone and fallen in love with him, and what am I going to do?

Help. Please. A miracle would be especially appreciated. Gotta go. Kisses.

Megan.

"He's coming over."

"When?"

"Now."

"What about your cast?"

Megan didn't meet June's disapproving gaze. "I'll get it off."

June moved in front of her, blocking the television, which Megan wasn't watching anyway. "When?"

"Soon."

"Megan, you have to tell him."

"I will.

"When?"

"Soon."

"Okay." June stepped away as she threw up her hands in disgust. "Have it your way. Don't tell him. Don't take off the cast. March forward in this wonderful, magical relationship that's built on a house of cards. It's your funeral."

Megan winced. Not just because her best friend was so ticked off, but because she was right. "Okay."

June opened the fridge and pulled out a green apple. "Okay, what?"

"I'll tell him."

"So you've said."

"No. I'll tell him tonight."

June, who'd just taken an enormous bite, stopped chewing and came back into what pretended to be a living room. "Really?"

Megan nodded. "I don't want to."

"I know, honey, but come on. He'll understand."

"No, he won't. And I won't blame him."

"If the situation was reversed, would you understand?"

"No. Maybe. Eventually."

"Right. Which is pretty much how I see tonight going. So don't get bummed if he's all hysterical about it. It's gonna take him some time. Just believe that whatever you two have together is enough."

"What if it isn't?"

"Then you need to know that, too."

"But..."

"I know."

"You don't." Megan stood up, put her crutches under her pits and walked over to the kitchen. She stared out the window, even though there was nothing to see but another brick building. "June, I'm in love with him."

"Well, duh."

She whirled around. At least as fast as a woman on crutches can whirl. "You knew?"

"I'm your best friend, dummy. Of course I knew. You're practically floating on air. You can't sit still. You're complexion is amazing."

"I didn't know until this morning."

"I never said you were particularly bright."

"Gee, thanks."

"You're welcome."

Megan headed toward the club chair where June had made herself comfy. "You don't think it's too fast?"

"Sure it is. But what difference does that make? If it's right, it's right."

"You believe in love at first sight? The woman who thinks all fairy tales should be banned from the planet?"

"Why not? What I don't believe in is fooling yourself. There are no perfect happy endings. That's a dangerous bunch of crap. But that doesn't mean there can't be enduring happiness."

"My goodness."

"What?"

"I'm so glad you're my friend."

June gave her the old raspberry, which was unfortunate, because she was still eating the damn apple, which was generously sprayed around the room.

Megan grimaced, but June thought it was hysterical. When she finally stopped laughing, she got up and gave Megan a big old hug. "I know it's going to be okay. Trust in yourself. You'll be fine."

"I'd better be."

June stepped back, gave her a once-over. "Is that what you're wearing?"

"I was. Why? Does it make my ass look huge?"

"No. I'm teasing. You look fabulous."

Megan hobbled over to the mirror she'd hung on the back of her bedroom door. She'd put on a skirt, a long one that covered her legs. Black velvet, it made her feel pretty, until now, that is. "Are you sure?"

"Yes. Jeez. I should know better than to tease someone in love."

Megan turned her gaze to meet June's. "It isn't fair, you know."

June nodded. "Yeah. Sometimes it sucks. But what can you do?"

"I see these models with their movie stars and their mansions and everything you could ever want, and they're not happy. Maybe one or two of them, but mostly, they're just as miserable as us mortals. So if they can't be happy..."

"Why should their genetic freakdom give them special privileges? No one gets by on a pass, Megan. No one."

"I know. Oh, God. How am I going to tell him?"

"Just give it to him straight. Don't pull any punches, and don't try and make it anything more than what it was. He was supposed to be a fling. Just like he wasn't supposed to ask you out on a second date."

"Okay. Wish me luck."

June came around and gave her a major hug. "It's gonna be fine. Call me if you need me. Wake me up if you have to."

"Thanks. You're the best."

"No, I'm not. I just want you to be happy."

"Why do I feel so miserable, then?"

"Stick to the truth. Tell him how you feel. It'll work out the way it's supposed to. Now, go I must. Tired, Yoda is."

Megan smiled as she watched her friend leave. The clock in the kitchen ticked away, bringing Luke closer. She loved him. And despite June's confidence, Megan knew in her heart she was going to lose him.

16

LUKE GOT TO HER PLACE just after seven. It was one
of those brownstone conversions that used to have
four really big, really beautiful apartments, with lots
of bedrooms and sitting rooms and baths. But then
developers got hold of it and split it into as many
units as they could without having the tenants actually sleeping in closets.

Megan lived on the second floor, and while there
was an elevator, he took the stairs. Her hallways had
decent lighting, but it still smelled like too many people in too small a space.

He ran a hand through his hair, checked the bouquet of flowers which had cost him a bundle, then he
knocked. He felt like a kid at Christmas, all because
he got to see her.

And there she was, holding the door open for him,
looking so pretty in her long skirt and sweater. She'd
worn her hair loose, and he decided this was the way
he liked it best. With her body balanced on those
damn crutches, he had to restrain himself, when he
wanted to scoop her up in his arms and carry her off
to the moon.

Instead, he held out the bouquet.

She sort of melted when she looked at the flowers.

"Oh, Luke, they're beautiful. How on earth did you find tulips this time of year?"

"I'm glad you like them."

"I do. Come in, come in. Let me get a vase."

He followed her inside, shrugged out of his coat and hung it on the coat tree just this side of the door. She turned, but he stopped her from leaving. "Not so fast," he said. Putting the flowers on the small table by the stove, he pulled her to him, held her steady with one hand while he put her crutches against the door with the other. When she was unencumbered and he had her full attention, he kissed her.

She sort of melted into him, which was even better than her reaction to his gift. Her body got soft as her arms went around his neck. She rubbed against him, her breasts on his chest, her velvet skirt brushing against his slacks.

He savored the taste of her, and when her tongue slipped between his lips, his cock swelled. He couldn't believe the effect she had on him. Thinking about her was bad enough, but being with her sent him out of control.

"I've missed you," he said as he moved to taste her in the sweet spot beneath her ear.

"You saw me last night."

"But I didn't get to do this," he said, nibbling her earlobe, making her tremble.

"Oh, right. This," she said, her voice dreamy and sweet. "What a terrible oversight."

"I know. We need to make up for it. Now."

"Umm, sounds perfect. Just let me put the flowers in water."

"The hell with the flowers," he said, as his hands

went down to cup her butt. He held her steady as he rubbed against her, making sure she understood the urgency of his request.

She shimmied against him, but then she pulled back. "It'll take two seconds to put them in water. They're beautiful and I love them, and you can just hold that thought."

He frowned. "All right. But I'm warning you. There could be dire consequences."

"Such as?"

"Honey, there's just no telling when this'll blow."

Her laughter made things, surprisingly, worse.

"Don't just stand there," he said, walking with her toward the kitchen. "Hurry."

She walked a bit lopsided, using him to lean on as she pulled a glass vase from above the sink. The water was rusty so that it had to run a few seconds before she could finish up. In the meantime, he did his part by cupping her breasts in either hand, holding her steady, so she wouldn't fall.

He chuckled. What a humanitarian he was.

"There," she said. She put the vase on the counter and dislodged his hands as she turned around. "Are you going to stand there all night, or are you going to undress me?"

"My mistake. Sorry."

"Okay, but don't let it happen again."

He saluted her, then took hold of her sweater and pulled it up over her head. She had on a black lace bra with low cups. The very edges of her nipples peeked above the material, begging him to lean over and lick them, then down farther, finding the nubs of her nipples. He didn't move the bra. Not yet. But he did suck each nipple, making sure they were as hard as they could get.

When he stood up again, he kissed her quickly on the lips. "Bedroom?"

She nodded to the left. The logistics of getting her into his arms were a little too sophisticated for his lust-addled brain, so he did what he had to. He grabbed her by the waist, hoisted her up, and over his shoulder.

"Hey!"

"Hang on. We're almost there."

She grabbed onto his waist as they walked. He felt her lace-cupped breasts on his back, the warmth of her breath lower still. It was impossible to resist the lure of her derriere so close. He nipped her through her skirt, patted her with his free hand.

Then they were in the bedroom, and he lowered her gently down. That was all he did gently. Once he could get at her, he turned her so her head was on the pillow, both legs on the bed. Crawling on himself, he maneuvered between her legs and tossed her skirt up. Panties. Black lace to match her bra. Pretty. But in the way.

He tugged them down, Megan obliging by lifting up just enough to slip them off. The cast gave him no trouble at all. He tossed the panties over the bed, took hold of her legs, and opened her like a present.

Even though his pants had grown very tight, he didn't adjust them or even take off his sweater. First, he needed to taste her.

Bending low, he ran his cheek over her soft, pale inner thigh. He must have still been chilly, because Megan gasped, her body jerking reflexively. Calming her with a soft, "Hush," he kissed her delicate skin, a soft touch of lips, a slow inhalation of her intoxicating scent. Another kiss, higher, and another. He took his time, battling his own urge to hurry, to ease his own ache inside her.

When he reached the downy softness between her legs, he nuzzled there, his tongue lapping in tiny swipes growing ever closer to the velvet wet heat.

Megan moaned, her body writhing now on the cushion of her comforter. He held her steady as if impatience got the better of him.

With his free hand, he petted her lower lips, heard her mewl, felt her fingers grip his hair, tugging slightly, but not pulling. He parted her and ran his tongue down lightly over what was revealed.

She tasted of sex and sin and sweetness, and it was all he could do to keep his touch feathery.

"Luke…"

He heard his name float above him, and then again. Torn, he decided to pause for a look. His reward was the abandon on her face, the flush on her cheeks, her moist lips parted and her breathing heavy with need.

As beautiful as she was, he wasn't finished with his task. He bent down again, closing his eyes, letting his senses guide him.

He found the bud of her clitoris, and as he touched it she tugged on his hair, arched up, straining. Teasing, he pulled back, keeping the pressure a constant, not letting her have her way just yet.

She settled and he licked hard, circling, circling, feeling her swell. Her thighs tensed, trembled. She let go of his hair but he heard her fingernails scramble on the smooth comforter, trying to find purchase.

Hardening his tongue, he went in for the kill. She had to orgasm soon, or that joke he'd told earlier would come true; he would explode, and dammit, he wasn't about to do that in his pants.

More pressure, high cries, inarticulate words. The bedcover pulled up off the sheets, his head sandwiched between her trembling thighs. He could hear his own breath echo in his ears, as if he were under water.

"God, God! Luke, wait, stop. Oh, God."

He didn't stop, of course, at least not right away. He took her beyond where she thought she could go, to a second spasm that knocked him loose. That was all the signal he needed. He sat up and practically ripped his clothes off.

She was no help. She just lay there, her skirt, in what was becoming something of a pattern, bunched around her waist. Her nipples still hidden behind the teasing black lace.

MEGAN WATCHED Luke strip as she recovered from his wicked tongue. She'd never come like this, never. Not even when it was just her and her vibrator. He transported her to someplace high, white, intense, and she wanted to go back as often as possible.

But now, she had another delight in front of her. His shirt was off, and his chest, all ripply and masculine, with just the perfect amount of dark hair, made her mouth water. How could one man be so scrumptious? She growled deep in her throat and pushed herself to a sitting position. The skirt had to go, and she wrestled with that as he undid his belt. His zipper came down as her skirt went over her head. When she could see again, he was pushing down his trousers.

She attended to her bra but fumbled a bit when his erection was freed. Her eyes widened. He was very, very ready.

"Come here," she said, surprised at how rough her voice sounded.

"One second." He scrambled off the bed, toed off his shoes, then stepped out of his trousers. A moment later he was back on the bed, on his knees, straddling her hips.

"Closer."

"Why?"

"There's something I need to do?"

He took hold of himself, hefting the weight of his engorged cock. "What would that be?"

"I can't tell you. I need to show you."

"Is it safe?"

She smiled. "Nope."

His grin was as wicked as her own as he inched his way up the bed until he was almost close enough.

She took his hand away, and took the hot flesh in her own hand, guiding it to the tip of her lips. A pearly bead of moisture hung on the very edge, and she slowly opened her mouth, stuck out her tongue, and licked it off.

He moaned, pressed forward. But what was good for the goose was good for the gander, and she held him back, determined to make this as torturously wonderful for him as he'd made it for her.

With a patience she could only muster because of her recent release, she circled the head of his cock with her tongue, amazed at the smooth silk of his flesh.

He provided a steady chorus of low groans as she worked her way up his shaft. She licked him everywhere leaving no spot untended. Her other hand cupped his testicles, gently bringing him so close she had access to all the family jewels.

"Please," he whispered.

She freed him from her mouth long enough to say, "Please, what?"

"Please let me inside you."

"You are inside me."

He leaned forward until his hands braced his upper body on the wall behind her. "I can't take this much longer."

She ignored his plea and took him as far back in her mouth as she could. He was large, too large for her to hold him completely, but she did pretty well. She sucked, hard, pulled back then forward, increasing the pressure and the friction until she felt his whole body tremble.

Enough. She wanted him inside her, and she wanted it to last. This was very likely the last time she'd be with him. The last time she'd make love. The thought, so successfully denied since he'd arrived, hit her with the power of a knockout punch.

She cried out, and he got very still. "Are you all right?"

She nodded. Ran her hands up his slender hips. "Make love to me," she whispered. "Please, Luke. Right now."

He moved so quickly she thought he might fall. Reaching across the bed, he plucked a condom from

the comforter that he must have dropped when he
undressed. He ripped the package with his teeth, then
sheathed himself with an ease, an elegance that was
extraordinary. But she closed her eyes because
watching him move made her terribly aware of her
own clumsiness. Even without the cast she could
never be like him. Never have that innate grace.

He gathered her in his arms, kissed her deeply,
then shifted until he'd nestled between her thighs.
She lifted her one good leg and wrapped it over his
back. She felt the blunt tip of his sex at her opening,
and she arched off the bed, impaling herself on him.

Crying out as if she'd hurt him, he thrust home,
filling her, making her whole. The kiss broke apart
as she gasped, incredible shivers and spasms shaking
every part of her body and a hundred prayers swam
in her head, incoherent yet perfectly clear, all asking
for the same thing.

To keep him.

To keep this.

He thrust again, and that was all. He came, pressing into her as if he could bury himself there forever.

All she could feel were her own tremors and the
tears inching down her cheeks.

LUKE WOKE UP at sunrise. It was a habit, one he
couldn't seem to shake even when he wanted to. Like
this morning. Thank God he didn't have to go to
work.

He had some errands to run, but none that couldn't
wait until this afternoon. Maybe Megan would like
to go to breakfast. He knew a great deli not far from

here. After, they could go to a movie. Or come back here and make love.

Of course, she might be a little sore today. He was. Not that that would stop him. Damn.

She was still sleeping, her hand curled up under her chin, her hair all wild and sexy. He shouldn't wake her. Not again.

Last night had been something of a marathon, with some breaks for food and naps until finally, about four this morning, they'd both cried uncle. She'd been a trouper, though. Willing to try just about anything.

He thought about when she'd brought out the Kama Sutra oil, and his poor little willy started to get hard again. Yeah. He was sore, all right.

Better to think of something else. Keep his mind off the incredibly soft woman sleeping inches away, all naked and sweet and—

Municipal bonds. That was the ticket. There was an article about munis in the *Journal* he'd meant to read. He'd do that first thing Monday morning. Kent Jones, one of his newer clients, would do well to buy some bonds, keep himself protected. The guy wanted to make money fast, but he didn't have the capitalization to get too risky.

Luke shifted over, punched the pillow a few times, wondered if he could fall asleep again. He wasn't a late-night guy. Never had been. His best hours were the early morning when he could get out and run on deserted streets, or get that first shot at fresh powder.

He closed his eyes, started his self-relaxation routine, starting with focusing on his toes, then his feet, his ankles, imagining them hollow, filled with a warm pale liquid.

He reached his knees, then Megan moved, her hand touching his back, and there went any plans of relaxation or sleep. Better to get up, maybe take a run around the block.... Shit. He hadn't brought sweats, and he wasn't about to run in his suit. Maybe he could dash home, grab a change of clothes, get back here before she woke up.

Hell of an idea. He turned to make sure she was still sleeping, and she was. Her lips had parted just a bit. Damn, but he liked kissing her. He liked doing everything to her, with her.

This was definitely no ordinary, run-of-the-mill infatuation. She'd gotten to him. What he didn't know was what it meant. He'd done little else but think about it in the past couple of days, and he was pretty sure he wanted this to keep on going. Of course, he might be kissing his perfect future goodbye, but maybe not.

He slipped out of bed, his feet cold on the hardwood floor of her bedroom. His clothes were all over the place, but he found everything before he headed for the john. If he hurried, he could be back here in forty-five minutes.

IT WAS THE EMPTINESS of the bed that woke her. A memory of the ski lodge, of the note he'd left her, made her stomach clench before she was truly awake. Her hand went to his pillow as she strained to hear a sound, any sound, in her apartment. All she heard was the whine of a garbage truck from down below.

Throwing back the covers, she sat up, swung her

legs over the side of the bed. It was cold. She got up, did that strange lopsided walk she'd gotten too used to on the way to her closet, and slipped on her old chenille robe.

Wondering where she'd find the note, she made her way into the kitchen. It was on the counter. Right next to the tulips.

Went to get clothes. Hoping you're still sleeping when I get back. I want to wake you. If not, how does deli sound?

　　　　　　　　　　　　　　　　Love, Luke

Her heart jump-started and she laughed out loud. He'd gone to get a change of clothes. That's all. And he wanted to have breakfast with her.

She clutched the note to her chest. *Love, Luke.* Was it possible he meant that? That it wasn't just a convention, a slip of the pen?

Moving over to the fridge to get the coffee, her gaze fell on a snapshot of her and June from two summers ago. They'd been fooling around at a mall in Teaneck, and had found one of those photo booths. She'd always loved the picture, but seeing June's smiling face was a sharp reminder of what she had to do when Luke returned.

Maybe, if *Love, Luke* was real, then there was a chance she could survive the day. Something told her not to get her hopes up.

Last night had been the most special of her whole life. It had transcended anything she'd ever known about being with another person. It was hard to explain, but something spiritual had happened to her.

Her heart had become something new. He'd merged with her, and now his loss was going to leave a hole that could never be filled again.

She got the coffee, went through the motions of making a pot, and every second that ticked by brought her further down. There was no easy way out of this, no words that would mitigate the situation. She'd lied. She'd pretended to be someone she wasn't. *Love, Luke* couldn't be true. Because how could he love someone he didn't know?

17

LUKE RACED UP the stairs to Megan's building, feeling oddly refreshed after running around in a mad attempt to make it back before his lady woke.

The effect was lost completely, however, as he stood outside her door, and realized he had no key. He'd have to wake her if he wanted to go back inside.

Shaking his head at his own foolishness, he knocked and was somewhat surprised when the door opened immediately. He grinned, happy to be back, happy she was up. Just happy.

"I'm such a lunkhead," he said, walking past her until she shut the door, then scooping her up in his arms. "Such great plans for one with no key."

He kissed her then, glad for her warmth, ready for the coffee he smelled just behind her. But something stopped him from grabbing a cup. Something stilted, stiff about Megan. He looked at her. She smiled, but it was off. "What's wrong?"

"Nothing," she said too quickly. She distanced herself, turned to the counter. "Coffee?"

"Sure," he said, "but not until you talk to me."

"About what?"

"I can tell something's wrong. Are you angry because I left? I tried damn hard to get here before you woke up."

"No, I'm not angry at all. Honestly. Maybe a little tired, still. Coffee will fix everything."

He doubted, but accepted the cup she gave him. He liked it black, and knew she used a packet of sweetener and milk. He also knew she liked tea, hot cocoa, some wine. She tolerated brandy and hated scotch. But there were a million things he didn't know about her. He wanted to uncover all her secrets, one at a time. He didn't seem to care how long it would take.

"You seem awfully chipper for a man who got three hours sleep."

"I know. I can't explain it." He sipped the coffee, then went to the living room and flopped on the couch. "I usually work out first thing in the morning. My body just hasn't caught up yet. I'll probably crash face-first in my eggs."

"I hope not."

"Hey," he said. "How come you're over there, and I'm over here?"

She fluttered her long lashes at him, and headed his way. She didn't have her crutches, but she seemed to be walking all right. "That doesn't hurt?"

"What?"

"Walking without the crutches."

"Oh." Her cheeks got pink for some reason, and she stopped en route to the couch to fuss with a potted ficus. "No, it doesn't hurt."

"That's great. That means it won't be long till you get it off, right? What did the doctor say?"

"Soon," she said. "Next week, maybe."

"Fantastic. We'll celebrate."

She glanced at him, smiled, then turned away. Now he was certain. Something was really wrong.

"Hey, Megan. Come here." He patted the seat beside him. "Please."

She nodded. Her chest rose and fell with a deep sigh. But she did come to him, and lowered herself carefully onto the couch.

He touched her chin, lifting it with his finger until her gaze met his. "Talk to me."

She opened her mouth, then shut it again. Swallowed. "Tell me again about your master plan."

He didn't get it. Why the question, why he was suddenly feeling like he'd missed the second act of this play. "What's this about?"

She shook her head. "Please. Tell me."

He drank a little more coffee, then decided to play along. Surely, he'd figure out the problem if he could just get her talking. "The plan is to retire when I'm between forty and forty-five. To get a place in the mountains where I can fish in the summer and ski in the winter. Oh, I've been meaning to ask. Do you like to fish?"

"I don't know."

"What? How can you not know?"

"I've never fished."

He gaped her at. "Are you serious?"

"Yes."

"Shit. It never dawned on me.... Well, I think you'll like it. I hope you'll like it."

Her gaze dropped again. "Go on."

"Oh, yeah. I've diversified my investments to hedge against inflation, and I've made sure I'm secured against anything less than total disaster. Not that I'm a hundred percent secure, but as close as I can get.''

''And a large part of the plan is to go solo, right? Until after you have it all together.''

He frowned, not liking the direction this conversation was taking. ''Yeah. That was the plan.''

''That *is* the plan. The plan you've had all your adult life. The plan you've built your dreams on.''

''True. But I've been thinking…''

''Me, too.'' She struggled to her feet, walked to the window and stared out. ''I don't want to be the one to ruin it for you.''

''Ruin it?''

She nodded. ''You've been totally straight with me, and I admire that. I wanted to… I mean, I… I have something to tell you.''

''What?''

She didn't say anything for a long time. Her hand went to her face, and even though he couldn't see, he felt sure she was wiping tears from her cheek.

''Megan?'' He stood, walked over to her. ''I don't understand.'' He touched her shoulder and she cringed. The move hit him like a blow.

''I've just thought about it, that's all. You've worked so hard. If you just keep on going, you'll have everything you've ever wanted. I won't let you risk that. Once you retire, then we can, you know, find each other again.''

''You're not serious.''

She turned to face him, and she didn't have to speak. He could see that she meant every word. ''Luke, it's for the best. I would hate it if you resented me for things going wrong. I couldn't live with that.''

''Who says things would go wrong?''

''Things never go exactly as we want them to. Even with the best intentions. People screw up.''

''I'm not going to lie and tell you I haven't been concerned about...this. Us. But dammit, Megan, I think we should give it a try. If it doesn't work out, oh, well. We'll live.''

She closed her eyes, but not in time to stop the tear from trickling down her cheek. ''I can't do it,'' she said, her voice barely above a whisper. ''I wish I could, but I can't. I'm sorry. I'm so sorry.'' Then she turned around, covered her face with her hands.

When he touched her, she shook him off. He tried again. She turned, but she wouldn't look at him. With her hands at her sides, her shoulders hunched and the saddest expression he'd ever seen, she said, ''I can't run away, Luke. Not with this cast on. So you'll have to be the one to do it for me. Please.''

''No, I—''

''Please. Don't make me beg.''

He couldn't have been more stunned. He'd been ready to change everything for her. He'd convinced himself she was worth it. Now, she wouldn't even try? She wouldn't even talk about it?

Maybe she was right. He'd been infatuated. It had clouded his thinking.

But dammit, this felt worse. Leaving her felt unbelievably wrong. He'd thought, on his way over this morning, that this might just be heading toward love. That alone should have warned him off.

No, man, something was wrong here. She was too

hurt, and the thought of never seeing her again was unacceptable. "Megan, don't do this."

She opened her mouth, but he put a hand up to stop her.

"I'm leaving, okay. I'll go. But don't make up your mind yet. Think about it. Let's talk tomorrow." He backed up, but as he did, he dug out his wallet and pulled out one of his business cards. "I'm just going to leave this on the table. You can reach me at this number any time. I'll forward it to my cell and my apartment. You call me, okay? And we'll figure this out."

"All right," she said.

He hit the door. "I just want to say one more thing."

She nodded.

"Figure out what's right for you. Not what's right for me. Okay?"

Her face screwed up, like she was going to burst into tears, but then she got it together. "Thank you, Luke. And just so you know, this has been the best time I've ever had. Ever."

"Yeah," he said. "Me, too. God dammit, Megan. Me, too." He turned then, and walked into her chilly hallway, closing the door behind him.

He'd never been hit by a truck. But he was damn sure this was what it felt like.

MEGAN BARELY MADE IT to the couch before she crumbled. She curled over until she was as small as she could be, and she let the sobs that had been building rack her body with tremors.

She was such a coward! How could she have been so weak, so stupid. God, oh, God.

He'd looked so hurt. Would the truth have been worse? Only for her. Weak, spineless her. Why had she ever come up with this ridiculous plan? She didn't deserve Luke. He was much better off without her.

He'd been willing to change his whole life for her. That was the horrible part. That he'd believed her to be good. Worthy. But she wasn't. The lie had grown too big, gotten completely out of hand.

If she called him right back, told him everything, it would still be hopelessly screwed up. He wants to spend his life fishing and skiing. With a crip? Oh, God. And what if she told him everything, and he was too embarrassed to tell her he didn't want to be with a cripple. That would be just like him. Noble. Kind. And wouldn't she just love saddling him with that kind of burden for the rest of his life.

She'd done the right thing. Horribly. In the worst way possible. But in the end, it was for the best.

As for her, she deserved the pain. It would hurt forever, and that was just the way it was supposed to be.

She sat up, found a napkin by the side of the couch and blew her nose. She had to call Darlene and get the damn cast off. Now, before she had second thoughts. Before she could call him and beg him to come back. But first, she'd call June. She needed reinforcement.

MEGAN OPENED her eyes and looked at her leg, freed at last from the synthetic cast. She cringed, hardly able to look. The real horror wasn't the hair, which was long enough to braid, or the fish-belly white skin tone. It was the misshapen, stick skinniness, the long ratcheted scars around her knee, her calf and her ankle. Evidence of unsuccessful surgeries that had left her with no hope at all of ever looking normal again.

June inhaled sharply. ''Whoa. That's going to take a couple of Lady Bics.''

Darlene laughed. ''It's so unfair. I want to know who invented this no-hair rule for girls? What kind of sick man decided we had to be the ones to shave.''

''Men shave their faces, and we don't have to.''

Darlene gave June an arch look. ''No? Wait till you hit menopause and tell me that again.''

June snorted as she bent to help Darlene pick up the pieces of the cast.

''Which reminds me,'' Darlene said. ''How did it work? Did you get your Man to Screw?''

Hot tears flooded Megan's eyes, and no matter how fast she blinked she couldn't hold them back. June was at her side in a heartbeat, holding her steady.

''What? What did I say?''

''It was a Man to Do,'' June said. ''And yeah, she got him. Only things didn't exactly turn out like she'd hoped.''

Darlene tossed a big chunk of cast in the garbage. ''Oh. Sorry.''

Megan smiled at her. She was really nice, and had been such a sport to do this. It wasn't her fault it had all gone to hell. ''I still owe you that drink,'' she said. ''I'll give you all the gory details then. But the short version is, we met, it was fabulous. The whole ploy worked like a charm. Only, just my luck, it turns out he's…'' She took a deep breath. She would *not* cry. ''…he's the one. The man of my dreams.''

''Why on earth would that be a problem?''

''Because I lied about my leg.''

''Big deal.''

June nodded. ''My point, exactly.''

''You don't understand.''

''What's to understand?'' Darlene said. ''If he's the right guy, then a little fib isn't going to stand in the way.''

''June, tell her.''

''Wait a minute,'' June said. She got up and sat across from Megan. Darlene's apartment was bigger than Megan's, and decorated with real furniture, not Salvation Army and flea market specials. She'd done it up in earth tones, which worked with her own low-key sense of style. Megan was in a brown leather chair; June perched on the arm of the matching sofa. ''Why do you think Luke liked you?''

''What?''

''He broke all his rules to be with you. Why do you suppose he did that?''

''Come on, don't be dense. He thought I was normal. Like all the other women at the lodge.''

''Oh, yeah. That makes sense. He broke his rules because you were interchangeable with every other woman there.''

Megan sniffed. ''So he liked the way I drew.''

''So that's what you two did all last night? Drew pictures?''

''No.''

''Come on, girl. You were in a cast, for God's

sake. He was at a lodge with tons of gorgeous babes who could ski. And yet..."

Megan blinked. "Oh."

"Yeah. Oh. You big dummy. The guy didn't fall in love with your leg. He fell in love with you."

"But he wouldn't have even looked at me if I'd worn my brace."

"How the hell do you know that?" June stood up, her normally pale face flushed with red. "It has nothing to do with your leg. It's never had anything to do with your leg. Can't you see that?"

"You're wrong. Dammit, I didn't make this up. Remember that guy Andy? How he dumped me like a hot coal the minute he found out I was in a brace? And what about that guy you set me up with. Steve? Don't tell me you didn't see his reaction. You were there. You saw."

"So some men are stupid. But not all of them. Not most of them. Megan, honey, I love you like a sister, but it's not your leg, it's how you feel about your leg that scares them off. You don't give them a chance to know you."

Megan sighed. "I wish that were true."

"It is true. You're scared of rejection, so you beat them all to the punch." June knelt in front of her, taking Megan's hand in hers. "You hide behind your leg, sweetie. Which is well and fine, except you're trading safety for happiness, and that's not a very good deal."

She stopped talking until Megan met her gaze.

"Take the risk. Go for it. You're already miserable, so if you're right, who cares?"

Megan stared at her friend for a long time.

LUKE SMILED as his date ordered. Salad, vinegar dressing on the side. Seared tuna, no oil, no potato. No bread. Champagne cocktail.

He held back a sigh and ordered himself the osso bucco, risotto, salad with blue cheese, half bottle of cabernet sauvignon.

The waiter left after a very European bow, and Luke turned his attention to Lauren. She was a copy editor at one of the big publishing houses, and she lived in Cal's building. Normally, Luke didn't mind being set up. He'd met a lot of nice women that way in the past, and expected he would again. He realized now, as he tried to think of something, anything, to say that perhaps a week after he and Megan had split up wasn't the best timing.

Split up. As if they'd been together. That was what got him. Of course, she hadn't called. He'd picked up the phone a dozen times to call her, and each time he'd forced himself to forget about it. So why in hell was he still thinking about her?

"Is something wrong?"

"Pardon?"

Lauren quirked her head, ran her finger around the rim of her water glass. "I get the feeling you'd rather not be here."

Shit. He hadn't realized he was so transparent. "I'm sorry. It's not you. I've had a pretty lousy week. I figured going out tonight would be perfect. I could forget about it, but now all I seem to want to do is rehash my mistakes."

She nodded. "I understand. I've been there. Would you like to do this another time?"

"No, no. I'm here now. I won't go there again. That is, if you're willing to give me another chance."

"Of course."

"So," he said, leaning back on the banquette, "what were you saying?"

"I mentioned that I had season tickets to this wonderful theater, The Roundabout. The last production was just terrific, a play by Richard Greenberg. Have you heard of him?"

"Yeah, I have. I've seen a couple of his plays."

He listened as she gave him a rundown on the plot. By the time she got to the third act, the salads arrived. He was hungry and the food was terrific. Lauren made him laugh, and she was actually quite bright. That, combined with her looks—she was a knockout, reminded him of Darryl Hannah—should have made the evening more than pleasant.

Only Megan was there, the whole damn night, poking at the back of his mind. He had to shake her. This was ridiculous. He'd figured out days ago that her reasons for pulling the plug on their relationship had little or nothing to do with his master plan. She'd changed her mind. Found something about him she didn't like. He doubted it was the sex, but who the hell knew?

Maybe that's why he couldn't let it go. The not knowing. It was driving him crazy.

Regardless, he didn't embarrass himself too much with Lauren, but he didn't pursue her, either. At the end of the night he was home, alone. And Megan, one more time, haunted his dreams.

18

MEGAN STARED at the telephone, and as she had every day for the past three weeks, she thought of calling Luke. Instead, she finished eating her tuna sandwich as she logged onto her Internet server. It was her first break of the day. Damian was working on his new spring line, and she'd been in his office most of the day. She'd done some nice stuff, going further on her own than she'd ever dared before. Miraculously, he'd complimented her on a couple of drawings. Not that he'd never done that before, but this was the first time he'd noticed that she'd taken off on his idea, expanding and interpreting based on her own concepts. Actually, it was the first time she'd been brave enough to show him her interpretations. He'd looked at her as if he'd never seen her before.

She'd been scared to death, but her courage had paid off. Not that he'd offered to make her an assistant designer or anything, but the seed that she was creative was planted, and she knew in her heart she was no longer just a walking pencil to him.

Instead of going right to her e-mail, she decided to take another risk. Why not? It was a time of risks. Beginning with the fact that she had worn her short skirt to work. It was black, tight and it showed off her legs. Both legs. Brace and all.

She'd waffled all morning, putting on the skirt, changing it to something longer, putting on pants, then back to the skirt. She'd driven herself crazy. In the end, she'd forced herself to wear it. She had on her clunky shoes with thick soles, her secondhand cashmere sweater and matching headband. According to June, she was da bomb. Phat city. She'd have to trust her on that, because she felt like her brace was lit up in neon.

The odd thing was, no one on the subway had given her brace a second look. No one at work had either. Gerry, the mail guy, had actually whistled at her, and she didn't believe he'd been making fun.

The trick was to act as if she felt like a babe. According to June and Oprah and Dr. Phil and all sorts of self-esteem gurus, acting as if was half the battle. In theory, she'd begun to believe it. Eventually, she wouldn't even have to fake it.

Okay, so it did feel good. The black tights helped, but she had to admit, the freedom was exhilarating. So, onward and upward.

She went to the Web site she'd found two weeks ago, only this time, she wasn't just going to read about it. She was going to sign up.

The page came up for the Adaptive Sports Foundation. Pictures of monoskis and disabled athletes made her heart beat faster as she searched for the registration link. She was going to do it. Learn how to ski. Risk breaking her other leg, making a fool of herself. She was going to step boldly outside her comfort zone.

The next class was going to be held just after New Year's. It would cost her a couple of hundred, but that's what savings accounts were for. June was going to have a cow when she found out.

Before she could change her mind, Megan filled in all the blanks and hit Send. She would be able to rent the equipment once she got to the upstate New York resort, and a coach would be assigned to assess her abilities. She wasn't going to be doing any slalom skiing, but maybe, just maybe, she'd get down a bunny slope without killing herself.

She smiled. This was a good thing. Even though it was also a very scary thing. She just wished she could tell Luke.

With the thought came the all too familiar blanket of sadness. Missing him had become the background noise of her life. Three weeks of thinking about what he'd meant to her, and how she wanted to live the rest of her life.

Three weeks of staring at his phone number, dialing and hanging up before it rang. Three weeks of the worst kind of torment.

As June said, if she was going to be in pain anyway, she might as well learn a lesson. He'd been a very hard lesson.

She'd been so close to happiness. Real happiness. But her fear had kept her standing on the outside looking in. It had taken awhile, but she'd finally understood that if she was ever to find that kind of love again, which was doubtful, she'd have to stop hiding behind her brace.

While the Men To Do project was fun, and in theory it made sense, she wasn't interested. She didn't want to *do* anyone. She wanted to love. And be loved. To share the important things. To be honest and brave and to face the real issues of her life.

So she had a lot to thank Luke for. She wished she could thank him in person. But that was a bravery outside her reach. Even though she rehearsed and re-hashed a hundred scenarios, going to Luke and telling him she'd lied was just plain too much for her. She was still on the bunny slopes, and confessing to him was expert all the way.

She went into her e-mail program. She'd learned that thinking too much about Luke was dangerous. Her heart hadn't started to heal yet. She wasn't sure it ever would.

Heather had written to suggest the new book for the group, one of the Sleeping Beauty books by Anne Rampling, a pseudonym for Anne Rice of Vampire Lestat fame. Megan said she'd be willing to give it a try, even though she'd heard some wild things about it. She just hoped by the time the final vote was in, it wouldn't kill her to read about all that sex.

Sex. Oh, God. It had been so incredible with Luke. Dammit, it was easier not knowing making love could be so wonderful. Now she had something con-crete to miss. Her bed had never felt so big and lonely.

The next e-mail was from Gretchen, and from the first line, Megan's spirits plummeted.

He's gone. Paul's gone, and he's taken everything from me. He wasn't a producer at all. How stupid could I be? God, I can't stop crying. I can't work, I can't sleep, I can't eat. I don't think I can survive this. He took it all. Wiped me out financially. I have to move back home, which I swear is going to kill

*me. My mother wants me to see her shrink. I'm afraid
they're going to lock me up. Maybe I should be put
away. It's a nightmare, and I can't wake up. He had
me completely fooled. He and his friends. They were
all in it together. I have no idea what his real name
is or where he lives. All I know is I gave him my
heart and he crushed it. Broke it beyond repair. I
trusted him. I trusted myself. I'm such a fool.*

*I probably won't be back. I can't afford e-mail
anymore. I'm sorry. I didn't mean to ruin it for everyone. I'm sorry.*

Megan wiped the tears from her eyes and read the
message again. Poor, poor Gretchen. It was too horrible. That bastard! Megan wondered if they could
trace him. Hire a private detective and find the son
of a bitch.

Liar.

Like her.

Shit. What a nightmare. She was tempted to blame
Men To Do, but she couldn't. Several of her friends
had had wonderful experiences with the Man To Do
project. And of course, the original women had met
their husbands that way. But for now, Megan was
going to stick to reading about relationships, not trying to find one. Not even a one-night stand. She
would concentrate on herself. Find out who she was,
and what she truly wanted from life.

In the meantime, she didn't have much time to
write to Gretchen. Her lunch would be over soon,
and she wanted to stay in Damian's good graces. She
hit Reply, and wondered if there were any words at
all that could help her heal. That could mend a broken heart.

She sure hadn't found them for herself.

"EXCUSE ME. I'm looking for Megan Hodges."

The guard, an elderly Hispanic man with an ill-fitting uniform and a shock of white hair, looked up from his paperback book. "Who?"

"Megan Hodges. She works for the House of Giselle."

"Yeah, okay. They're on the fifth floor. You need to sign in before you can go up."

Luke wrote his name on the guest log. "Any idea where on the fifth floor?"

"Don't know. It's a lot of people up there."

"Okay, thanks." He went to the bank of elevators and pressed the button. Under normal circumstances, he would have enjoyed looking around the building. It was highly stylized, built in the 20s or 30s, and he was a big fan of the art, but he was too busy thinking about what he was going to do once he got to her floor.

The thing was, he couldn't get her out of his head. He'd tried. He'd focused on the market, on his portfolio, he'd gone out on a few dates, he'd worked out so hard he'd strained his back. Thoughts of Megan popped up at the oddest times. He kept thinking he saw her in a crowd, crossing the street. He actually stopped a woman coming out of Bloomingdale's.

It made no sense. He wasn't the kind of guy to fall in love. Frankly, he'd always considered himself too selfish. But that's the only explanation he could come up with.

The elevator door opened, and he stepped inside. He was alone until the third floor where two women joined him, both attractive, both with very friendly smiles. He just nodded politely until he reached his destination. It had been like that for three weeks. He wasn't interested in anyone. Anyone but Megan.

The reception desk on her floor was empty. Behind the smoked glass desk was a logo for the House of Giselle, so he knew he was in the right place. He just had to find her. Assuming he'd caught her on the right day.

He crossed the foyer and went down a long hallway. Pictures of famous models and fashion magazine covers plastered the walls, but the doors had no signs on them. He saw one woman on a cellphone, but she disappeared behind a cubicle before he could catch her attention. Then, as he almost reached the end of the road, a tall man in a floor-length white fur coat stepped into the hall. Luke hurried over before he could disappear. "I'm looking for Megan Hodges."

The man seemed startled, and he looked Luke over from head to foot. He didn't seem impressed. "I don't work here." The accent was British. Hyde Park, not Liverpool.

"Oh, sorry." Luke headed down the hall again, but the Englishman called out.

"I'm not sure it's who you're after, but I may know her. She's the girl with the leg brace, right?"

Luke shook his head. "No. She did have a cast on, though."

"A cast? No, sorry. This girl, she's crippled. Awful sort of metal contraption on her right leg, I believe. She's Damian's assistant illustrator."

Crippled? That wasn't right. But then, the guy

didn't really work there, so he probably had it wrong. Luke doubted there could be two Megans who worked for Damian. "Can you tell me where to find her?"

"I think so." He pointed down the hall, in the opposite direction. "Second door past the elevators. Make a right. Keep walking until you see a picture of Cindy Crawford in a string bikini. Megan's office is the first door on the left."

Luke thanked the man as he retraced his steps. The directions were clear and it didn't take him long to find the bikini picture. The first door on the left was closed. But he hesitated, before he opened it, wondering if he was making a mistake.

Megan could have called him, but she hadn't. He'd thought of a million reasons she'd cut him loose, everything from a psycho ex-husband to a terminal illness. It drove him crazy, and the bottom line was, he couldn't stand it. He had to know. Maybe if he understood, he could let it go. Let her go.

Or maybe she'd worked out whatever the hell problem she had and she'd be glad to see him. They could pick things up right where they'd left them. He wasn't counting on it. But he sure was hoping.

He took off his gloves and stuffed them in his coat pockets. Ran a hand through his hair. And then he walked through the door.

MEGAN STUDIED the dress on the bust, trying to figure out what she didn't like. The lines were good, the material flowed well, but something was off. The color? The print? The darts?

She tore off her last drawing, crumpling the paper

and throwing it into the large wastebasket beside Damian's work stand. She wasn't ready to draw yet. Not until she figured this out.

"I hate it," Damian said.

"I don't hate it." She walked to her right, looking at it from a different angle. "But I don't love it."

"I hate it," he said again. He took a long swig from his herbal chai, and tossed his hair back dramatically. "Take it down."

"Hold it," she said. "What if you raised the waist? Made it more like this?" She adjusted the dress on the mannequin. It was better, but still not a winner.

"I don't know." Damian walked around to the back. "It's hideous from here. Who are you?"

Megan looked up to see her boss staring behind her. She turned to see who'd come in, and her heart stopped. "Luke."

He stared at her as if he'd never seen her before, his gaze fixed on her leg. On her brace. On her lie.

"What happened?"

"I can explain," she said, desperately searching for a way to make him understand. She barely registered Damian's quick departure.

"I thought you broke it."

She wanted to hide, to shield him from the disfigured limb that looked so unlike her healthy leg. "It was just for the week. So I could pretend—"

"He said you were crippled. I told him he was wrong." He looked up from her leg, met her gaze. She saw the moment he understood the truth. When the lie became real and painful. "You said you hit a tree."

"I know. I said that because of this stupid game. An experiment. I never expected to see you again."

"You lied to me."

"I know. But it wasn't supposed to be like this. I didn't mean to hurt you."

"So you really didn't care about my plans or anything, did you?"

She took a step toward him, but he backed up as if he couldn't bear her to be near. "I did. I do. I'd just got caught up in this…thing. You were supposed to be my Man To Do."

"What?"

She shook her head, cursing her own stupidity. She had to explain. He'd come for her. Come back after she'd told him goodbye. She couldn't lose him again. "Nothing. It's nothing. I just, I thought it was harmless. I wanted to feel—"

"I had it all wrong," he said. "Shit. I'm such an ass. I was going to change the whole thing. The whole master plan. I had it all worked out."

"Please," she begged. "Let's sit down. Let's talk about it. I swear—"

He shook his head. "I made a mistake. I won't bother you again."

"No, please!"

But he was already at the door.

She went after him, into the hallway. "Luke!"

He didn't stop. He didn't even pause.

"Luke," she whispered, but she couldn't see him through her tears. "Please. I'm sorry. I can explain."

The hallway was empty. It was over. Fool that she was, she'd thought her heart couldn't hurt any worse than the night she'd told him goodbye.

19

"IF YOU COULD HAVE seen the look on his face,"
Megan said, her tissue wet with tears, her cheeks
damp and hot with shame. "Oh, God, June, he
looked so horrified."

June sighed, rubbed her face with the flat of her
hand. "Oh, man. I can't believe it. If only—"

"Yeah," Megan said. "If only. I could have called
him. I could have explained it somehow. I never expected him to come back." Her throat closed again
as she agonized, as she catalogued mistake after mistake after mistake. He'd come for her. He'd found
her. And she'd blown it beyond any hope of re-
demption.

"Go see him. Explain it to him. From the beginning."

"As if he'd ever want to see me again."

"He obviously cares about you. Why else would
he have come to your office?"

"He might have cared. June, it's over. Done. I've
screwed everything up." Sobs bent her in half, made
it impossible to speak or even breathe.

"Megan, look. If he heard the whole story, he'd
get over it."

"You didn't see him."

"I know." June got up off her couch and crouched

in front of Megan. She took her hand, gripped it tightly. "Do you love him?"

Megan sniffed. Nodded.

"Then fight for him. Give it another chance. Don't regret not trying."

"Come on, June. There's nothing left to try. He hates me."

"No, he doesn't. He doesn't understand."

"I don't either. Dammit, why did I have to wear this stupid skirt. If I'd worn something else, he'd never have known."

"He would have, honey. Eventually. So the timing was bad, don't let that be the end of it."

Megan stared at her hand, still entwined with June's. She felt a cavernous emptiness, a despair that swallowed everything. "You know what I did about an hour before he showed up? Talk about irony."

"What?"

She looked up. "I signed up to take skiing lessons."

June bit her lower lip, and Megan wasn't sure if it was to stop herself from crying or laughing.

"I wanted to tell him that he'd changed me. That being with him had been the best thing that ever happened to me. I kept rehearsing what I'd say. I figured, if I could just find the right words."

June stood up. She pushed her hair back and took the scrunchy from around her wrist and put her red curls in a ponytail. She'd been out running in her old thrift shop sweats. Megan had found her just outside the building. When June had seen her face, she'd dragged her up to her apartment, poured her a shot of whiskey and made her tell all.

"Forget about the right words," she said, crossing over to the kitchen and getting down a juice glass. "If you wait for the perfect words, you'll wait forever. Just tell him what happened, as if you were telling me."

"I can't."

June poured herself two fingers of whiskey, then went back to sit on the couch. She curled her legs under her and leaned forward. "Yes, you can. Dammit, Megan, do you want him or not?"

"Of course I want him."

"Then get over yourself and go find him." She tossed back the whiskey, shivered dramatically, then looked Megan in the eyes. "What in hell do you have to lose?"

"I STILL CAN'T believe it." Luke leaned back in the leather booth. The bar, small, crowded with stockbrokers and secretaries, felt stuffy with all the winter coats hanging limply by the front door. If he hadn't been sitting with Cal, he would have walked out, walked anywhere. Instead, he drank his scotch and wallowed in his own misery.

"What did she say?"

"She said it was some kind of game. That she never expected to see me again."

"Hmm."

Luke looked at his friend, not liking the direction he seemed headed in. "What?"

"I don't know. Maybe she had a good reason. It doesn't seem to me like you gave her a chance to explain."

"Explain what? That she met me under false pretenses? That she lied her ass off?"

"Yeah. That."

"Are you high?"

"No. I just think you should find out the whole story."

Luke grunted his disgust. "She's a liar, Cal. What else do I need to know?"

"Well, for starters, that you haven't been able to get her off your mind. That she's the first woman ever that made you consider changing your damn master plan. That you haven't been the same since you met her."

Luke blinked, not believing what he'd heard. "What part of liar don't you understand?"

"Screw that. She met you on vacation. Everybody does shit like that on vacation."

"I don't."

Cal gave him a withering look. "You've got your own issues, buddy boy."

"What the hell is that supposed to mean?"

"Look." Cal leaned forward as someone cranked up the juke box. The Police screamed out "Every Breath You Take." "Let me ask you something, and dammit, you'd better be straight with me. Would you have given her a second look if you'd seen that brace? If you knew she was disabled?"

Luke opened his mouth for a smart-ass retort, then closed it again. Shit. He thought about that first night he'd seen her, sitting with her drawing pad, her broken leg bolstered on the ottoman.

If she hadn't had the cast on, would he have talked to her?

He wanted to think he would, but the truth wasn't so generous. He would have walked right by her. Not that it would have repulsed him or anything half so strong, he just wouldn't have put her in the playmate category.

What did that say about him? That he was a callous, superficial bastard? Maybe.

"I'm not judging here," Cal said. "I don't know. I probably would have walked past her, too."

Luke closed his eyes for a long minute. When he opened them again, the bar seemed even more crowded. He didn't want to be here.

"Dammit, Cal, I wanted her to be part of it."

"Part of what? Your plan?"

He nodded. "I figured, together, we could still make it happen. Only, we'd concentrate on her dreams, too. I know a hell of a lot about the fashion industry now. I could write a book."

"What now? Are you going to drop it?"

"Hell, yes. Okay, I see your point about her leg, but that doesn't change the fact that she lied. She had plenty of opportunities to tell me what was going on. Instead, she made me believe she was breaking up for my sake."

"Maybe she was. Maybe she couldn't see you being with her if you knew she couldn't keep up with you."

"You don't know that. People ski who've lost their legs. She could have done it if she wanted to."

"Really?"

Luke narrowed his eyes and tried to see past Cal's studied indifference. "How come you're on her side? You never even met her."

"I'm not on her side, as you so maturely put it. But I've seen you mope around for three weeks, and buddy, it ain't been pretty. I've also been the one who's had to listen to you talk about her and talk about her. Face it, she got to you. She broke through."

"But that's when I thought I knew her."

"What's changed?"

"Aside from the whole lying thing?"

"What if, just for argument's sake, we suppose that she had good reasons for what she did. That you could get past it. Would you still want her?"

Luke stared at a woman standing just past the booth. Tall, slender, beautiful. She was just the kind of woman he'd have pursued before he met Megan. Just the kind of woman he'd have slept with and never called again. Whole, healthy. If he'd met her at the lodge, she'd have been great for an evening's entertainment. Just like all the other women he'd met.

Until Megan.

But that didn't change the facts. She'd lied. She'd tricked him.

"Do you love her?" Cal asked.

"I don't know," he said.

"Then you'd better figure it out."

MEGAN STARED UP at Luke's apartment building, shielding her eyes from the chilling rain. It was late, too late for her to be standing here, and certainly too late for her to go up and knock. He would be asleep by now.

Yet she didn't try to flag down a cab or even head to the subway she'd taken to get here. This part of town was unfamiliar to her, being so close to Wall Street and all. The building looked old, but nice. No graffiti on the walls. A doorman behind a big wooden desk.

Cold water trickled down her neck, underneath her sweater. She shivered, praying for courage she didn't feel. The weekend had passed, and she'd been immobilized with sadness. Despite June's encouragement, she hadn't been able to get herself out of her funk, not even to go to work this morning.

She had to try. Even if he threw her out on her butt, she had to tell him the whole story. Not for her sake so much as his. She couldn't let him think he'd been a dope. Gullible. She'd tricked him, and none of it was his fault. He'd done nothing to deserve this.

She wiped the rain from her eyes and goaded herself forward. No one else on the glistening street, arcs of pale light in pools marking the long block. Inside the building looked warm and inviting, and she was so terribly cold.

She stood for a moment before grabbing hold of the heavy glass door and pulling it open. At the sound, the doorman looked up. He seemed surprised to see anyone out on such a nasty night.

Her heels clicked on the tiled floor, echoed against the concrete walls. As she got to the desk, the doorman, his uniform old but nicely pressed, put aside a copy of *National Geographic*.

"Can I help you, young lady?" His voice was kind and deep, and so were his eyes.

"I'm here to see Luke Webster."

"Kind of late for a visit, isn't it?"

She nodded, and she wished he wouldn't ask her

any more questions. Her throat was swollen with tears.

"Does he know you're coming by?"

She shook her head. "We had a fight."

"Ah, I see."

"It was my fault." She sniffed, ran a wet sleeve under her nose. "I was awful."

"And you want to make it right?"

"Yes, sir."

"I'll need to call up, you know. I'm not allowed to let you go up without permission."

"I understand."

"You wait right there. Try and get warmed up." He lifted a phone, pressed some numbers. Then they waited for what seemed like forever, the big clock behind his desk ticking long past midnight.

"Mr. Webster? Sorry to disturb you, sir. It's George from downstairs. There's a young lady here. Dripping wet. Says she's come to patch things up."

Megan closed her eyes. She couldn't bear to see the look on George's face when Luke told him to get rid of her. The words would come soon enough.

"Yes, sir," he said, and she realized he sounded just like James Earl Jones.

The click of the phone on the table startled her into opening her eyes. George's warm smile reassured her instantly. "He says to come on up. He's in twelve-ten. Up the elevator to your right."

She took a deep breath, her fear of facing Luke ten times worse than the fear of being sent away. Damn her for being such a chicken. Hadn't he taught her anything. "Thank you," she said, her voice barely above a croak.

"It's gonna be fine," he said. "Don't you worry. Mr. Webster is a good man."

"I know," she said. Then she turned and headed for the elevator. The walk was endless, and yet she was inside the cab too fast. She wasn't ready. She didn't have the words.

June had told her over and over not to rehearse. Just to tell him the truth. What June didn't seem to realize is the truth sucked.

She pressed the button, and the doors whooshed closed. It was nice in the elevator, much nicer than at her place, which always seemed to smell like wet dog, even though pets weren't allowed. She almost expected music, but she rode alone with her thoughts. Her heart beat so hard against her chest she felt it might break through.

No such luck. She arrived at the twelfth floor in one piece, still dripping, her clothes underneath her coat as soaked as if she'd been standing in the shower. It didn't matter. Nothing did, but taking one step, then another. Her feet silent on the dark carpet, her shadow from the wall sconces as jerky as her unsteady gait.

He stood by his door. As she drew closer, she could see she had awakened him. His hair was all mussed, his robe tied haphazardly over sweats. No slippers.

She stopped a foot away. "Hi," she said.

He looked at her for a long time. "You're all wet."

She nodded.

Again, he just stared. It was torturously hard not

to run. To let him see her dripping in humiliation. Finally, he stepped back. "Come on in."

She moved slowly, careful not to brush him with her coat. Inside, there were only a couple of lights on, so she couldn't see much. It was big for New York. She could see a big-screen TV in a nice-sized living room, along with a leather couch and chair. He had books. Lots of them.

The door closed, and she winced at the sound. God, she was really here. She had no idea what to do.

"I'll warm up some coffee," he said. "Why don't you take off your coat."

She obeyed, letting the coat fall in a puddle at her feet. Her shivering actually got worse now that her wet sweater and skirt were exposed to the air. She crossed her arms in front of her, hugging herself, although it didn't help much.

"Shit, you're soaked," he said, and she could hear the hint of disgust.

"I shouldn't have come," she said, bending to pick up her coat. His hand on her arm made her freeze.

"Come on, come with me. We have to get you out of those wet things."

Like a child, she followed him down a hallway to his bedroom. Inside, she saw his bed. It was really big, like the one at the lodge, with a dark comforter and pillows. It was too dark to see much more, only what the lights from the building across the way illuminated.

He opened his closet door and disappeared inside for a moment. He came back with a pair of sweats, some color she couldn't see with the lights out. "You can put these on. I'll go finish the coffee."

She nodded. He left, closing the door behind him.

Moving in slow motion, she pulled off the sagging sweater. She folded it and put it on a chair she didn't think the wet would ruin. Her bra hadn't fared much better than the sweater, so she took that off, too.

Her skirt followed, and by then, she was shivering so hard her teeth chattered. All she wanted to do was put on those warm sweats, drink something hot. No, that wasn't true. All she really wanted was a miracle.

She took off her shoes, her arm brushing against her brace. It was so damn cold.

She stood up slowly and as she turned, she caught sight of herself in his mirror. Stringy wet hair, skinny pale body and the leg. Her hated leg.

This is what she was trying to hide. What she thought was so ugly. Oddly, even with the rain still dripping off her nose, she felt a kind of peace as she stared at herself. She wasn't that horrible. Not really. It seemed foolish, all of a sudden, to have cared so much about such a little thing.

She turned slowly so she could see herself completely. Even though the light was dim, she saw more than she ever had before. It was as if she was seeing through new eyes.

Bending carefully, she undid her brace, sliding it off her leg and laying it beside her. She stood once more, and this time, there was nothing between her and the truth.

Her leg was smaller than the other. There were scars around the knee and ankle. A bend that shouldn't be there. She leaned a bit, and her foot turned at too sharp an angle.

She looked for a long time. When she was ready, as ready as she'd ever been in her life, she limped to the door. She didn't take the sweats. She took nothing. Not even her brace.

With hands at her sides, she walked down the hall to the kitchen. Luke saw her as he poured a cup of steaming coffee. His eyes widened and he put everything down. "Megan—"

"This is me," she said. "All of me." She took another step toward him, so he couldn't help but see the limp, the asymmetry. "When I was a senior in high school, I was driving with my mother in her car. A drunk driver slammed into us on the Long Island Expressway. We rolled several times. My mother was killed. My leg was shattered. They had to use the jaws of life to get me out of the car. I was in surgery for nearly fourteen hours. I can walk at all because the surgeon was very, very good.

"When I woke up, it was to a different world. My mother was gone, and all I had left was my aunt and uncle. Oh, and my fiancé, Jeff. I ended up living with my relatives. Jeff didn't stick around.

"They tried to fix what was wrong with my leg. This is the best they were able to do. At least I'm not in a wheelchair."

"Megan—"

She held up her hand. "Please, let me finish. I don't know if I can get through it if I stop."

He nodded. She wished she could see his eyes more clearly. It didn't matter. This was all she had. The whole truth.

"I was as crushed as my leg when he left. I blamed the accident. My leg. I went to art school and got my degree, and I even got the job at the House of Giselle, and that should have made me happy, but I wasn't. I was too busy being self-conscious. I was sure all my problems were caused by my crippled leg.

"I hid behind my brace, Luke. I took no responsibility for my life. And then my friends heard about this wild scheme. It was called Men To Do. The theory was, that each of us in this online reader's group would find a man to do before we settled down. Someone scary or different. Someone we'd never have for keeps. I'm the one that came up with the cast idea. I figured I could pretend to be normal if my leg was in a cast. People would just think I'd broken my leg, but I wouldn't be *different,* you know? I'd fit in. And I'd see if the reason I didn't have a lot of dates was really because of my leg.

"I met you the first night. And voilà. I had my proof. It was my leg. You were so wonderful. I think I fell in love with you that first night. I wanted to stay there forever. I couldn't believe you wanted me, too.

"I was also absolutely certain that if you knew who I really was, you'd run the other way. I believed that the only reason we got together at all was because you didn't know about my real condition. That's why I didn't tell you. I was afraid. And selfish. And embarrassed."

"Can I say something now?"

She nodded.

"First, you're freezing to death." He undid his belt and took off his robe. He came up to her, and swung it around her shoulders. Then he brought it snug around her.

"Second," he said, and now she could see his eyes. The light from the living room hit at the perfect angle. "Second, I can't believe the kind of guts it took for you to do this."

"I know. Pretty amazing, huh?"

He nodded. "I think you're right about me. I hate to admit it, but I probably wouldn't have come up to you if I'd seen you in your brace. I'm not proud of it, but it's true. I'm pretty damn shallow, which isn't something I'm real thrilled about."

"At least you're honest."

"Sometimes. I've done a lot of thinking since Friday. I decided that I was going to call you. I wanted to hear what really happened."

"Oh?" she asked, her heart afraid to hear the next sentence.

"Yeah. Because, and this is as honest as I know how to be..."

She closed her eyes tight, waiting.

"Truth," he said. "I love you."

Her eyes opened. Wide. "What?"

"I think I fell in love with you that first night, too. Imagine that. Me. The cynic with big plans."

"You did?"

"Yeah. And the more I got to know you, the worse it got. Dammit, girl, I changed my master plan for you."

"Oh."

"I'm glad you told me what happened. And I have to admit, I'm glad you wore the cast, because if you hadn't, we wouldn't be here right now. And Megan..."

"Yes?"

"I dare you..."

"Dare me to what?"

"Kiss me. Stay with me."

She nodded once, and then his lips were on hers.

Epilogue

The following December...

LUKE STOOD at the bottom of the White Way ski run at Windham, looking up the mountain. The bright winter sky made him shield his eyes with his hand.

Bill Highland, Megan's ski instructor, shook his head. "She's going to be fine," he said. "She's co-ordinated and she's got a great sense of balance. Relax."

"Relax," Luke repeated. "Right."

"Look," Bill said, pointing. "There she is."

Luke shifted his gaze until he found her, Megan, identifiable as much for her outrigger ski poles as her bright red down jacket and matching pants. It was her first solo run, and his heart beat so heavily in his chest he thought he might need oxygen.

"Look, she's doing great."

Luke nodded. She was doing great. She'd insisted on taking her classes alone while he skied his Grand Slalom, and then she'd insisted on taking this run by herself. He'd loaded her onto the ski lift a half hour ago, and he hadn't been able to calm down since. If anything happened to her...

"Whoa, excellent! Did you see that? She took that mogul like a champ."

Luke had seen, and while he was as impressed as Bill, he wasn't going to celebrate until she was at his side. Safe. Damn, he'd never been this scared when he'd skied, not even his first time on the Super G.

She'd changed everything, dammit, and now he couldn't go back. The life he had before held no appeal. Together, they'd come up with a new plan, one where Megan could pursue her dreams, and Luke could still take early retirement. Maybe not at forty, but close enough. Besides, it wasn't so important anymore. What mattered to him now was Megan.

It had been her idea to honeymoon at the ski resort. Her insistence that she take the classes in adaptive skiing they offered here. He'd told her again and again he didn't care if she skied or not, but she was adamant.

Bill, one of the instructors who'd been specially trained to work with disabled skiers, had taken a shine to Megan, and he'd given her a few hours of private lessons this morning in preparation for her maiden voyage. Luke knew he had a class waiting for him by the Wheelhouse Lodge. But the man wasn't going anywhere. Not yet.

"Come on, babe," Luke whispered as the hill got steeper and her speed increased. She leaned to her right, using the outrigger for balance and friction. Damn, she looked great. He wished he could see her face. See if she was having fun, or if this whole thing had been a mistake.

"Okay, here it comes," Bill said.

He meant the second mogul. It was a jump, one he would have taken without pause, but significant for a beginner. He held his breath.

She hit the mogul, went into the air, and then his heart stopped. She twisted sideways, and he knew she was going to plow. Dammit! He should have gone with her. If she got hurt—

"Ouch," Bill said, then he sucked air between his teeth in a slow whistle.

Megan came down hard on her butt. One of the outriggers flew up in the air. She slid, snow billowing around her, blocking her from Luke's vision for too long.

"The hell with this," he said, then he turned to get to the closest lift.

A hand on his shoulder stopped him. "Wait," Bill said. "Let her do this."

"She could be hurt."

"If she is, we'll take care of her. But she's probably fine. It wasn't a bad spill. She needs to get up by herself."

Luke knew he was right, but he didn't know if he could sit back and watch. "It was stupid," he said. "She's only got one good leg."

"That's why it's so important," Bill said. "Trust me. I teach the adaptive course every winter. It's about the most liberating thing these people ever find. Let her be."

Luke kept himself still through sheer effort of will. "Come on, girl. Get up."

One of her outrigger poles moved, then the other, and a second later, Megan sat up. She wiped her goggles and her mouth, then planted her poles while she struggled to her feet. There. She was upright, and nothing looked broken. He still didn't want her up there alone. What if she was scared? Aching?

"There's your answer," Highland said.

Luke saw what he meant. Megan had clearly spotted them. She stood sideways so she wouldn't slide down, and shook her poles over her head.

"Still worried about her?"

Luke had to smile. She was waving her arms like she'd just finished first at the Olympics. Then she got in position again and headed down the run.

He felt so proud he wanted to burst. "No, I'm not worried about her. She's one hell of a trouper."

"You got that right." Bill held out his hand, and Luke shook it. "She'll be fine. Let her know if she wants to go to the advanced class, she's ready."

"I will."

"I've got some people waiting. You tell her she did great."

"Thanks again."

Bill nodded, then pushed off toward the lodge, leaving Luke to wait for Megan. He didn't have to wait long.

She glided down the hill, steady, strong, like she'd been skiing her whole damn life. He saw her grin from a hundred yards off, and when she smashed into him, it was everything he could do to keep them both upright.

He felt her quiver, and then the sound of her laughter echoed off the mountains. "Did you see? Was I fabulous or what?"

"I saw, I saw."

"But I fell and then I got up, and it didn't hurt, except for my butt, but that's okay, because I did it! I came down the mountain. I want to do it again. Can I?"

Luke laughed. Just looking at the joy in her face, the way she bounced up and down in her eagerness to share, made him feel foolish for his worry.

"You want to go again now?"

She nodded, pushed her goggles back so he could see her eyes. "Luke, it's so cool. How did I not know this? Skiing is just…just…"

"Fantastic."

"Yeah."

He kissed the tip of her cold, pink nose. "You know what else is fantastic?"

"What?"

"You."

Her grin broadened. "You're just saying that because I'm the queen of the ski slopes."

"No. I'm just saying that because it's true."

"So you aren't having second thoughts about marrying me?"

"Not yet."

She kissed his lips, his cheek. "Cool."

"Now, are you *sure* you want to take another run? Cause I was thinking…"

"What?"

"We have that big old Jacuzzi tub in the room, and that nice bottle of brandy."

Megan looked up the mountain, then back at Luke. "What the hell," she said. "I can ski any old time."

"Besides," he said, letting her go so they could make their way to the tram that would take them to the lodge. "We've got to continue with my research."

"Ah, yes. Sex positions for those with a leg brace. Very critical."

"I think so."

"Ah, the sacrifices I make for science."

He bumped her with his hip. "Sacrifices?"

Megan tried to keep a straight face, but it wasn't possible. God, she loved him so much. Today was just another example of how he'd changed her. How he'd given her a life she'd never dreamed possible. "Hey, Luke?"

"Yes?"

"I think you should know that I love you very much."

"Really?"

"Uh-huh."

"How much?"

"Come on, ski boy. I'll show you." She pushed off, feeling strong and proud and free, her husband right behind her. Truth was, she was the luckiest woman in the whole wide world.

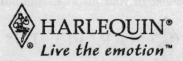

HARLEQUIN® Temptation.

AMERICAN HEROES

**These men are heroes—
strong, fearless...
And impossible to resist!**

Join bestselling authors Lori Foster, Donna Kauffman
and Jill Shalvis as they deliver up

MEN OF COURAGE

Harlequin anthology
May 2003

Followed by *American Heroes* miniseries
in Harlequin Temptation

**RILEY by Lori Foster
June 2003**

**SEAN by Donna Kauffman
July 2003**

**LUKE by Jill Shalvis
August 2003**

Don't miss this sexy new miniseries by some of
Temptation's hottest authors!

Available at your favorite retail outlet.

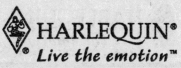

HARLEQUIN®
Live the emotion™

Visit us at www.eHarlequin.com

HTA

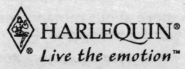

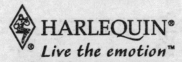

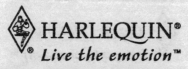

HARLEQUIN® *Blaze*™

Rory Carmichael is a good girl, trying to survive the suburbs.
Micki Carmichael is a bad girl, trying to survive the streets.
Both are about to receive an invitation
they won't be able to refuse....

INVITATIONS TO SEDUCTION

Enjoy this Blazing duo by fan favorite
Julie Elizabeth Leto:

#92—LOOKING FOR TROUBLE
June 2003

#100—UP TO NO GOOD
August 2003

And don't forget to pick up

INVITATIONS TO SEDUCTION

the 2003 Blaze collection
by Vicki Lewis Thompson,
Carly Phillips and Janelle Denison
Available July 2003

Summers can't get any hotter than this!

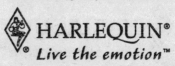

HARLEQUIN®
Live the emotion™

Visit us at www.eHarlequin.com   HBJE